Lock Down Publications and Ca$h Presents

Love in the Trenches 2 Playin' for Keeps

By: Corey Robinson

First Edition October 2023

Printed in the United States of America

Lock Down Publications
P.O. Box 944
Stockbridge, GA 30281
www.lockdownpublications.com

Like our page on Facebook: Lock Down Publications
www.facebook.com/lockdownpublications.ldp

Stay Connected with Us!

Text LOCKDOWN to 22828 to stay up-to-date with new
releases, sneak peaks, contests and more...
Or CLICK HERE to sign up.
Like our page on Facebook:
Lock Down Publications: Facebook
Join Lock Down Publications/The New Era Reading Group
Visit our website:
www.lockdownpublications.com
Follow us on Instagram:
Lock Down Publications: Instagram
Email Us: We want to hear from you!

This book goes out to "Pimpin 352"
Florida's next G.O.A.T. in the rap game.

Corey Robinson

Chapter One

Jarell stood by and listened to the heated exchange between the mocha-colored beauty and who he assumed was her man. He didn't know what had gone down to cause the drama between them, but he knew it had to be serious.

"You know what, Bak? Fuck you. I'm done with your no-good ass. I don't need this shit, and I don't have to put up with it. I'm a good girl, and I deserve so much better."

"Oh, yeah? Well, take your ungrateful ass on then but I can assure you that you ain't gon' ever find another nigga like me. I'm one of a kind, baby."

"Well, then, I guess we'll just have to see about that."

Alanee Travis had met M'Baku Reynolds her senior year of high school. She was a good girl who had big dreams of going to college and being someone important in the world, but she had been smitten with the streets' new up and comer and changed her whole outlook on the future. With his dark skin, natty dreds, big ego, and even bigger dick, he had been hard to resist. Countless other women threw themselves at him, but it was her that he had chosen.

She had never been a gold digger, but she liked the fact that he spoiled her with name brand clothes, expensive jewelry, and red bottomed heels. On top of that, her hair and nails stayed on point. There wasn't a bitch around who could touch her. However, she was blind to the fact that she was sharing the spotlight with others. Even when her best friend, Erica, tried to tell her, she refused to listen.

"I'm telling you, Alanee, that nigga ain't shit. Why you think he wants to keep you cooped up in that big ass condo by yourself all the time? His big ass been spending some of that hood wealth on other hoes. You ain't the only one. Shit, them throw away bitches living better than you."

Alanee always put it off as Erica being jealous because she had been the one to notice Bak first, but he wasn't feeling her like that and tried to pass her off to his partner, Brightman. She would never admit it, but Erica had been salty when she found out they had hooked up. Alanee had asked her about it one day, but she would always deny it.

"Erica, are you sure that you don't feel no type of way because Bak chose me? I mean, I know you're the one who saw him first and all. I just don't want there to be no kind of tension between us. That's all."

"What? I can't believe you would ask me that. You're my best friend, Alanee, and I would never allow a nigga to come between us. Especially one that ain't no good. You know me better than that."

"Well, it's gotta be something because you stay bashing him. Just tell me what the problem is."

"It ain't bashing him when everything I tell you is the truth. You so damn blinded by your feelings for him, but he don't care about your feelings when he's out with them other bitches. It's all good though. You ain't gotta listen to me but don't look for my shoulder when your tears start falling."

'You know what, Erica? I think you should find your own man to worry about, so you can leave mine the hell alone."

"Bitch, unlike you, I don't need a man. I got these fingers and a silver bullet that does the job just fine."

Alanee sucked her teeth and rolled her eyes at her friend. She knew that no matter what they said to one another, their friendship would remain intact. She knew that Erica only had her best interest at heart, but when it came to M'Baku, no one could tell her shit. She would just have to find out things on her own, and until that day came around, she would stick by his side.

"Eww, Erica. You are so nasty. I can't believe that you actually play with yourself, but now that I know, bitch, you better keep those hands far away from me."

"Now come on, Lanee. You mean to tell me that you don't pleasure yourself? Bak ain't never asked you to do it for him?"

"Hell no. Why should he have to ask me to play in my own pussy? That's what his Black ass is for."

"Well, there it is. That explains why his ass goes to other bitches. Men love that freaky shit in the bedroom. Your lame ass better get with the program if you tryin' to keep a nigga like Bak."

"Uh, thanks for the advice but I've managed to keep Bak for five years now with no problem so go head on with that shit you talking."

"Okay, since you've managed to keep him for five years, you wanna explain to me how he has a two-year-old son with Gina?"

"Nice try, Erica, but everybody knows that's Brightman's son. Try somebody else."

"Oh, so that's what he told you? Your ass will believe anything if you believe that, but it's cool. You still my girl even though you blinded by the dick. Come on and let's go get something to eat. Trying to make you see the truth has made a bitch real hungry."

The two friends shared a laugh at Erica's comment, but even though Alanee laughed on the outside, she knew on the inside that there was some truth in what she'd said. She had caught Bak a couple of times being unfaithful, but he always promised it would never happen again. She wanted to believe him, but the rumors she continued to hear made her doubt his word. She knew that she had been blinded, even when the truth was right in front of her. Erica's voice broke her from her thoughts and brought her back to reality.

"Lanee, damn. Where the hell is your mind at? I hope it ain't on that sorry ass nigga you call a man because I can assure you that his mind ain't on you. Now snap out of it and order your food. The man is waiting."

Alanee looked at her friend and then noticed the man that stood by the table with a pen and pad in his hand. She looked his six-foot stature up and down and raised her brows. She had always favored dark skinned brothers, but his smooth, light skin was flawless.

His neatly trimmed goatee was razor sharp, and his short fade was adorned with small curls that looked to be as smooth as silk. She wondered what it would feel like to run her fingers through them. She didn't understand why someone so fine was wasting his time waiting tables instead of slanging rocks on the block. He was thuggish in his own way, but she couldn't afford to waste her time on a nine to five nigga. She let out a long sigh and gave him her order. After he wrote it down, he continued to stand there and stare at her until she became annoyed by his presence.

"Uh, is there something else you need? You're making me feel some type of way by just standing there, staring at me. Shouldn't you be going to fill our order?"

He cleared his throat and got rid of what was on his chest. "Sorry bout that, Ma. I ain't trying to be rude, but your pretty face had me paralyzed, and I just couldn't will myself away."

"Well, I sure hope that ain't no pickup line because it was lame as hell. Besides, I already got a man, so you can carry on."

He nodded his head and walked away, cutting his losses. Erica shook her head and crossed her arms over her chest. She couldn't believe Alanee had been so rude to him, and she told her just how she felt.

"Now, why did you have to be so rude to him? That nigga was fine, and you just threw him away like he was a piece of garbage. You crazy if you don't get his number."

"Why in the hell would I want his number? His table waiting, broke ass can't do a thing for me. And did you forget that I already have a man?"

"You got something, but he's far from a man. And when in the hell did you become a gold digger?"

"Wanting a man with deep pockets does not make me a gold digger. His ass is in here waiting tables for a living. You can't really expect me to downgrade like that now that I've become accustomed to the finer things in life. Bitch, I belong on a baller's arm, and he clearly is not one."

"How can you say that when you don't know shit about him? This might just be something he does to clean his money."

"Erica, wake up. Niggas don't wait on tables to clean their money. They invest in businesses and pay other people to run them while they sit back and enjoy the fruits of their labor. Shit, you like him so much, you holla at him."

"Shhh, here he comes with our food. I think you've shot him down enough for one night."

The waiter made it back to their table and placed their food in front of them. He tried hard not to steal another glance at the mocha skinned beauty, but he just couldn't help himself. He didn't care about the attitude she gave him because it only turned him on more. He liked a woman who didn't mind standing up for herself. He needed someone just like her in his life.

"Okay. you're staring at me again, and I really don't like it, so could you please just go away? Your services are no longer needed."

Instead of walking off, he held out his hand and introduced himself. "Jarell Karter."

"Excuse me."

"My name is Jarell Karter and don't be mad at me because you so damn pretty. Blame that shit on God."

Alanee reached her hand out to shake his. She had to admit his admiration for her was flattering, but he just wasn't in her league. She couldn't get past the uniform he had on. She was attracted to niggas that wore starched up Polo jeans dropped just below their waist with the Polo shirt to match. What could he possibly bring to her life on a waiter's salary? He probably couldn't even take her out to eat from the tips he made. She hated to hurt his feelings, but what other choice did she have?

"Thanks, but I already told you I got a man, so you can save all those boring ass compliments for a bitch who needs to hear them. My nigga tells me I'm pretty all the time, so I already know it."

"Oh, yeah, well, let me spit something real to you. A man can tell you what you wanna hear all the time, but until he can show you, his words don't mean shit."

Alanee had been thrown off by his comment and had no clue how to respond. She looked to Erica for help, but she just shrugged her shoulders and continued to eat her meal. The truth was when she first met Bak, he complimented her all the time, but as the years passed, the compliments began to disappear. Lately, the only time he paid her any real attention was when he was deep inside of her. Jarell had clearly put her on the spot and left her speechless, but when he noticed, he at least bailed her out.

"It's all good, Ma. You ain't gotta comment on that, but if you ever want to be shown instead of just told, give me a call. I'll make sure I'm always available for you." He wrote his number down on a blank tab and laid it on the table in front of her. He would leave it up to her to decide if she wanted to pick it up or not. "Oh, yeah, your meal has been paid for. Have a nice night, ladies."

As soon as he walked away, Erica dropped her fork and stated, "Bitch, I'm going to eat out with you all the time. It's nice not having to pay for my meal for once. Especially one so expensive. We are definitely coming back here."

"Shut up, Erica. He probably had to use his employee discount to pay for it. His ass was just trying to impress me, but I didn't pay him any attention. I'm sure Bak has more money in the ashtray of his STS than that nigga has in the bank."

"Well, you sure didn't hesitate to pick up that piece of paper with his number on it and slide it in your purse."

"Whatever. Come on and let's get out of here. I'm tired and full and just wanna take a hot bath and lie my ass down. You know a girl like me needs her beauty rest."

The two women stood and made their way to the exit without a care in the world. Erica watched as Alanee slowly sashayed in front of her and shook her head. She had changed so much since she got with Bak, and even though Alanee wouldn't admit it, the change took a toll on their friendship. Erica didn't have a man in the streets. In fact, Erica didn't have a man at all. She was thankful the meal had been paid for because she could use the money on something else. She hadn't been able to live the big bank lifestyle like her friend and was doing all she could to keep up with her. M'Baku was a dog ass nigga, but he kept Alanee's pocketbook laced the fuck up. So far, Erica had been able to keep her envy at bay. She may not have been as thick or even as exotic as Alanee, but she was no scrub either. She also wasn't as boring as her friend was in the bedroom.

She kept it freaky, so a nigga would always come back, and knew that the old saying, "what one won't do, the next one will," rang true. She had noticed Bak checking out her fat print lately and made sure to wear tight jeans, so she could entice him even more. She didn't want to betray Alanee, but she figured that if she could get her to leave him alone, he would be fair game, and then, she could make her move.

"So, are you gonna call that sexy ass waiter? I know you didn't pick up that piece of paper just to look at it."

"No, Erica. I'm not going to call him. What could he possibly bring to my life? I already deal with enough drama, and you know Bak ain't going for that shit, talking about he's just a friend. I think you should call him instead and try to hook up."

"Uh uh, bitch. You ain't putting his ass off on me. Besides, it ain't me he's interested in, and you can say what you want, but I could have swore I saw a little sparkle in your eyes when you looked at him. I haven't seen you look that way in a really long time."

"I'll admit he was fine, but he ain't got shit to bring to the table but trays of food. I am not about to downgrade and make myself look like a clown. Bak spoils me and gives me whatever I want. I'd be a fool to fuck that up. Jarell ain't gonna be able to do anything for me off of those tips he makes. I would end up being the laughingstock of the block."

"Since when have you cared about what others say? Put yourself out there and see what happens. You might actually enjoy yourself with him. Bak don't be wanting you to go out because he don't want you to catch him with the next bitch, but you deserve to have some freedom too."

"You sure are trying really hard to put me in a bad situation. Kinda makes me feel like you got some motives of your own. What's up with that?"

"Nothing is up. You're my best friend, Lanee, and I just wanna see you with someone who deserves you."

"And how would you know if Jarell deserves me? You don't know his ass either."

"You're right. I don't know him, but what I do know is that Bak ain't shit. You've been locked down with him for five years and still in the same place you have been since day one. Exploring other options ain't gonna hurt you. I mean, Bak has explored other things. Why can't you?"

Alanee thought about what she said and hated the fact that she was right. Erica didn't know about the times that she had caught Bak out with someone else. She didn't want her to know all the bullshit Bak put her through on a daily basis, so she defended him every single time. The truth was that Alanee was ashamed of how he had done her, and yet, she continued to hold on, hoping that things could one day change. Deep inside, she knew that it would only get worse.

She finally pulled into the housing complex that Erica stayed in with her mother. She loved Erica, but she had enough of her for one night and couldn't wait to drop her off, but before she got out, Erica had one more thing to say. "Look, Lanee, just think about all I've said and go from there and call that fine ass nigga before someone else does."

"Okay, I'll think about calling him, but that's the best I can do. I'm not making any promises."

"That's enough for me. I'll see you later."

Alanee didn't pull off until Erica went inside and shut the door. She hated that her friend lived in section eight housing while she lounged in a two-story condo that Bak had put her up in. She had thought about asking Erica if she wanted to stay with her in the three-bedroom, three and a half bath abode because Bak hardly ever stayed there, but she wasn't sure she could handle her twenty-four seven, no matter how much love she held for her.

Her mind drifted to thoughts of M'Baku. She knew he had some kind of feelings for her but wasn't sure just how deep they ran. She couldn't understand why it was so hard for a street nigga to keep shit real, but she knew it came with the territory. She had the sudden urge to want to pick up her cell phone and call him. She wanted him to know just how she felt, but he told her that he had to go out of town on business, and she didn't want to disturb him. Then, another thought came to her mind and caused her to drive across town. She ended up on the street Gina lived on, and when she drove by her house, she soon regretted it.

"That bastard. Erica was right."

She couldn't believe that Bak's Caddy STS was parked in Gina's driveway. He had lied and cheated on her so many times but to have a baby by another bitch was the final straw. The tears formed in her eyes, but she had never been the type to cause a scene, and she wasn't about to change up. She sucked up her tears and turned around, so she could drive home and drown herself in the pitiful loneliness of her life. She pulled into the driveway and got out slowly, so she could assess the situation. She had gotten used to sleeping alone, but she had grown tired of it. She lied down on the couch because her broken heart wouldn't carry her any further, but before she closed her eyes, she pulled out the tab from the restaurant and held it tightly in her grasp, and then, she fell asleep.

Chapter Two

Jarell Ahmeek Karter had been born the son of a boss and was considered street royalty. His father, Janahvi, had been in the dope game all of his life, and while Jarell was growing up, he taught him everything he needed to know about the streets, but Jarell never had the desire to be a dope boy. It was just something that didn't appeal to him. However, he took in the ways of a gangster with ease. He decided to use it as a backup plan, just in case he ever needed one. Jarell knew that he could run with the most thuggish and still blend in with the business class. He was no fool though. He moved quietly and always kept a weapon handy because one could never be too careful, no matter the profession.

His uncle, Meek, had let his guard down and ended up with a bullet to the dome. Jarell's parents, Janahvi and Ashley, had kept Meek's spirit alive by naming their son after him and sharing the details of the legacy he left behind. He had gone out of town to handle a delivery with a cat he had dealt with many times, but it ended up being a set up. Meek had been gunned down before Jarell was born, but he felt like he knew him personally. He couldn't help but respect the love and loyalty that Meek had held for his parents. After his death, Janahvi had pulled back from the dope game, but it only lasted for so long.

Janahvi became bored because the streets were all he had ever known and teaching his only son the ins and outs kept him hungry for more. It wasn't the same without Meek, but he still managed just fine. Janahvi wasn't directly involved in the daily transactions, but he still ran the show, and before any money landed in his lap, it was washed and hung out to dry. Ashley kept hope that he would one day grow tired and retire from the streets for real, but no matter what he chose, her love never faltered, and she stuck right by his side.

Jarell enjoyed the stories of his parents' love, and no matter how many obstacles stood in their way or how much drama befell them, they held on to what they believed in and were still in love many years later. Jarell had always thought his mother was the perfect woman, and he hoped to one day find one that could fill her shoes. He had been unsuccessful until he met the woman at the restaurant who belonged to someone else. He remembered the day he overheard the argument between her and her boyfriend but wasn't sure exactly what it had been about. He wasn't worried though because Jarell wasn't about to let another man stand in his way. He felt something for her right away, and there was no way he would ignore it.

"Excuse me. I'd like a table please."

The voice brought Jarell out of his thoughts. He knew who it belonged to before he even turned around. Somehow, he already felt like she'd be back. He just hadn't expected her so soon. He turned around and smelled her sweet scent. Her red Chanel jumpsuit ate her curves up and caused his dick to react. He had been thankful for the apron he had on because he didn't want to offend her in any way.

"Well, well, well. Wasn't you just here last night? Either you like very expensive meals or you came back to stare a real nigga in the face. I'm kinda hoping it's the latter. Am I right?"

Alanee couldn't help but laugh, something she definitely needed. She was still trying to get over the fact that Bak had lied to her about going out of town, just so he could chill with the next bitch. She felt so humiliated because she had chosen to ignore all the signs. She couldn't help but jump to conclusions, something she usually didn't do. She needed an explanation and was going to confront him.

"Actually, I do like expensive food, but I'm really here to meet up with my boyfriend. However, seeing you might have had something to do with the location."

"Guess I was able to accomplish one thing I set out to do then."

"And what's the other thing?"

Jarell stepped a little closer, and when he noticed that she didn't move away, he knew that he had some type of chance with her. "The other thing is to make you mine, and for some reason, I feel like I'm going to accomplish that also."

"Don't get overconfident because I'm not that easy to obtain. Now, can you show me to my table? My man will be here shortly."

Jarell held his hands up in surrender and backed away, just as another waiter showed up. He turned to them and nodded. "Trevor, could you show this pretty lady to a private booth. She'll be expecting a guest so make sure you prepare it for two."

"Sure thing, Mr. Karter. Right this way, ma'am."

Alanee scrunched her eyebrows and pressed her lips together in confusion. She wondered why the other waiter had called Jarell Mr. Karter, but before she had a chance to question it, Jarell turned to walk away. His shoulders had her thinking real hard because she'd heard that niggas with broad shoulders could put down in the bedroom. He had her wondering just how true it was. Bak had been the only man she had ever been with, but Jarell had her thinking of trying something new.

She followed behind the waiter as he led her to a corner booth. She sat down and thanked him, and as soon as he walked off, Jarell walked back up and sat down in front of her.

"Look, I apologize for being so rude to you last night. I know that it was uncalled for. I'd like to start over. My name is Alanee Travis."

"Well, Miss Alanee, I do accept your apology, but that shit you talked to me didn't even faze me. I'm just glad to see you again, even if it has to be with your man. You seem like you got some deep shit going on in that pretty little head of yours. You wanna tell me about it?"

Alanee didn't know Jarell like that, but for some reason, she felt like she could pour her heart out to him. Her eyes watered, and no matter how hard she tried to keep the tears at bay, her broken heart wouldn't let her.

"Erica was right. I saw Bak's car in front of Gina's house. His Black ass lied to me and told me he had to go out of town on business, but his ass went to her instead. He is such a piece of shit."

"Whoa, shawty. Dry that shit up. You too damn pretty to be over here crying over some no-good ass nigga." Jarell placed a finger under her chin and gently pushed her head up, so he could look in her eyes. He couldn't understand how any man could make such a sparkling gem feel so dull inside. "Yo, Ma, don't you ever let a man make you feel like you gotta hang your head and look down. Any man that does that don't deserve you. No matter what he puts on your shoulders, you gotta remain strong and hold that shit up as high as you can. You a queen, and queens are supposed to always keep it together. How you think a king keeps his power? His strength comes from her. Now let me see that smile that had me in a daze when I first saw it."

A Kool-Aid smile spread across her perfectly glossed lips. She hated to admit it, but Jarell moved something inside of her. He made her feel like somebody but then again so had Bak when they first started out, and the thought pissed her off. She pushed his hand away from her face and leaned back.

"Look, Bak will be here soon, so you should probably get up and leave. I shouldn't have even put my emotions off on you. I mean, I don't even know you like that."

Jarell raised his brows at the sudden change in her demeanor and at the sound of Bak's name once again. He wondered if it was the same Bak his cousin, Trameeka, had been fucking with. The name wasn't a common one, and he was willing to bet a grip that the two were actually one in the same. He didn't want to say anything until he checked things out for himself and verified the information. He would make it his business to call his cousin as soon as he got a chance.

"I don't know why you so worried about your nigga when you can do so much better. If you was mine, I'd treasure you like a rare diamond, and each and every part of you would shine."

"Well, that's probably never going to happen. I'm sorry if it seems like I gave you some sort of hope, and please don't take offense, but dating someone who waits tables for a living ain't on my bucket list of things to do."

"You sho got a lot against a nigga who waits on tables."

"No, I really don't mean it like that. I understand you gotta do what you need to do, so you can live, but you can't expect a girl like me to waste my time on someone with a dead-end job. I mean, there can't possibly be a future in this kind of work."

"Damn, you don't mind dissin a nigga and making him feel like shit, do you? And furthermore, I have more of a future than a nigga in the streets, so maybe it should be your man you dissin instead."

"I'm sorry. I didn't mean to be so blunt but let's keep Bak out of this because you don't know shit about him. I always felt like it was best to keep things real from the jump. We can still be cool as long as you don't expect anything more from me."

"Sure 'preciate the honesty but you still could have been a little easier on me."

Jarell stood and towered over Alanee's small but thick frame. He turned to walk away, but she reached out and grabbed his hand and stopped him in his tracks. The connection caused chills to crawl up her spine, and she let go of him quickly.

"I'm sorry. I really shouldn't have said those things to you. I'm just hurting and a little confused right now, and it caused me to lash out on you even though you don't deserve it. You have been nothing but nice to me and here I go treating you like shit because of what someone else done to me. Can you forgive me?"

"You sure been doing a lot of apologizing, but I'll tell you what. I'll forgive you under one condition. You come hang out with me one night, no strings attached. If you don't enjoy yourself, I'll never bother you again. Ya never know though. It might just change your mind about waiters."

Alanee thought about it for a minute. It wasn't like she would be giving up the goodies, and she could use the change of pace. Plus, she was really feeling Jarell's vibe, but she knew she had to be careful because he was someone she could easily fall in sync with.

"Okay. It's a deal. But you better be more entertaining than your job makes you, and you better impress me."

"I would like to think that I already have, and speaking of my job, I met you because of it, and you ended up being the best tip I ever could have gotten."

Alanee caught herself smiling again at his choice of words. She tried hard to remember a time when she had been so happy, but nothing came to her.

"Okay, you can stop with the flattering now. I don't know what's taking Bak so long, but my ass is hungry, and I don't think I can wait any longer."

"Don't worry. I got you. I'll be right back."

Jarell walked off and went straight to the office of the restaurant and pulled out his cell phone. He sat down at the desk and called a piece of his heart. Trameeka Johnson was the daughter of his Uncle Meek and Auntie Tracey, but he loved her like she was his own sister. She was a year older than him, and he would pop slugs to protect her, even though he knew he didn't have to. Meek had been killed when Trameeka was only two weeks old, so she never got to know him. She had to depend on photos and tales of his life, but she loved him just the same. As soon as she picked the phone up, Jarell hit her with the questions.

"Sup, cuz. You still fuckin with that nigga, Bak?"

"Well, hello to you too and why are you asking me about him? Is there something going on that I need to know about?"

"Nah, just heard his name in random conversation. That's all. Nothing for you to worry about."

"Now, why do I feel like you're not telling me everything? Come on, Jarell, keep that shit one thousand. We family, so if I need to be put up on something, spit it out."

The one thing Jarell had never been able to do was lie to her, and he wasn't about to start, so he told her everything. "I met this chick I'm really feeling, but she keeps talking bout a nigga named Bak. She seem like she been fucking with him a long time. She's actually here at the restaurant right now, waiting on him, but something's telling me that he ain't gonna show. Her name is Alanee Travis. You ever heard him or anyone else in his circle mention her before?"

"No. I can't recall ever hearing her name mentioned, but you know how I am. I don't have the time to trip on a nigga about other bitches. I get mine, get paid, and send the nigga on his way. I know better than to catch feelings, no matter how good the dick is. That emotional shit ain't me at all. You already know my heart is six feet deep. Is there something you need me to handle this way? If so, you know all you gotta do is say the word, and it's done."

"Nah, ain't nothin'. At least not yet. I just needed to know if it's the same mufucka, but I already got a feeling that it is."

"You know I'm here if you need me, cuz. And speaking of Bak, that bastard just pulled up in my driveway. I'll call you back later."

Trameeka hung up the phone and left Jarell with a dial tone. He knew that she could stand up to the hardest of niggas, so he wasn't too worried. His cousin was truly a female gangster and could bust a gun without any fear in her heart. She was known for dogging out the niggas the same way they dogged out the women. Jarell knew that Trameeka's heart died along with her father. He couldn't remember a time when she was easy on anybody but family. Jarell's main concern was how Bak would act once she questioned him. He knew that once that nigga became paranoid, he was libel to do anything.

He slid his phone back into the pocket of his Polo jeans and tried to figure out how he would tell Alanee that Bak wasn't coming, but then he decided that he wouldn't tell her at all. He would just have to comfort her when she realized it. He walked into the kitchen area, so he could get the best chef in the state of Georgia to fix her a hot meal, but he noticed that the staff was cleaning everything up. He hadn't even realized how the time had flown by, but the thought of being completely alone with the beauty made his heart pound a little faster. He made it back to the booth he had left her sitting in and saw that she was in her own world. He knew that she was lost in the heartbreak that the next nigga had put on her, and all he wanted to do was make things right for her.

He didn't understand why women fell for the wrong men, and if what he suspected was true, Alanee's heart would be completely shattered, and Jarell would make damn sure he was there to put the pieces back together.

Chapter Three

M'Baku Reynolds felt like he had his shit together. He had started out in the dope game when he was fourteen years old, and that was also when he met his right hand, Brightman. Together, the two of them soared to greater heights and amassed a small fortune, along with street status. It wasn't major, but it was enough to put their names on the map.

Bak never really had much growing up. In fact, he didn't have shit. He'd never known who his father was, and when he asked his mother, she shooed him away because she honestly had no clue. She had slept with plenty of men, sometimes on a daily basis, and even after she became pregnant with Bak, she continued to do so. His mother had tried hard to make ends meet but having a habit made it difficult. When young Bak realized it was drugs eating up her money, it made him want to get on his grind.

He'd met Brightman while he was out on the block one night, and the two instantly clicked. When Brightman found out that Bak and his mother were living out the back of a car that didn't even run, he talked to his grandmother and convinced her to let them stay in the small guest house that sat in her backyard. It wasn't much, but it was warm and comfortable and much better than the backseat. Not long after, Bak came in from the block and found his mother dead from an overdose. He knew that after he'd lost her, he would never be the same. He could no longer bear to stay in the same room his mother died in, so he ended up moving into the main house with Brightman and his grandmother. Kevin King was given the name Brightman not because of the color of his red skin but because of the immense knowledge he carried around in his head. He had always been a good kid and made good grades, but when both of his parents died in a house fire while he was at school one day, his whole life had been turned upside down. He began skipping classes and making bad grades until he eventually got kicked out. After that, he threw himself into the street life and never once looked back.

Brightman sold dope like a real boss, but his real passion was in taking lives, and he prided himself on being the best gun in town. Bak liked the fact that his best friend could bring the muscle when someone fell short with his dough or tried him, which happened more often than not. The streets respected no one, not even a baller like M'Baku Reynolds.

"Aye, bruh, ain't you supposed to be meeting Lanee for dinner?"

"She'll be alright. I'll just tell her that something important came up, and I couldn't make it."

"Nigga, you my dawg and all, but you do Lanee foul as fuck."

"How bout you worry about your own bitch and let me worry about mine? Just chill out for a minute. I need to run in here and take care of something."

Bak pulled up in front of Trameeka's house and parked. He tried to make it his business to see her at least twice a week. He would make sure Brightman was with him, so he would have an excuse to not stay long, and it always seemed to work.

"Damn, Bak, why you had to bring your boy? You know I can't stand his red ass. How you expect me to concentrate on the dick with him sitting in my driveway?"

Trameeka had expected Bak and answered the door in her money green, La Perla lace bra with the panties to match. Her heart shaped, diamond, chopard earrings hung from her earlobes, and her money green Chanel pumps accented her freshly painted toes. Trameeka knew she looked fuck me ready, but Brightman ruined everything. He waved to her from the front seat of Bak's ride and caused her to roll her eyes. She had asked Bak on several occasions not to bring him when he came by, but he just didn't listen. She knew that it was an excuse for him to be able to rush out and meet up with the next bitch, but little did he know, the next bitch could have him because his dick game was getting annoying. He reached out and pulled her close and put his lips to hers, but as soon as they made contact, she pushed him away.

"Uh uh, nigga, why the hell do your lips smell like pussy that ain't mine? You could have at least brushed your teeth after you ate the hoe. You are so damn disrespectful, Bak."

"Oh, yeah? Then why yo' ass still fucking with me?"

"Because I know a good thing when I got it. Boy, I ain't trying to let all that dick go."

"Mmm hum, then come on and let a nigga slide real quick."

"Nah, fuck you. Why you always wanna run to me after you leave Gina's stank ass? And don't tell me that's not where you have been because that's her rotten ass pussy on your lips. You need to take that bitch to the doctor and get that shit checked out."

"That shit ain't true, Meeka. You know I don't fuck with her no more like that. The only reason I go by there is to see my son."

"I guess that's what you tell Alanee and all your other bitches, but I ain't trying to hear it because that shit is getting old."

Bak looked at Trameeka sideways because he couldn't believe she had mentioned Alanee's name. True enough, she knew about all the other ones, but he tried his best to keep Alanee out of the loop. He didn't even take her to the same restaurants and boutiques he took his other women. She hadn't been tarnished like the rest of them, and he wanted to keep it that way. He decided that if he ever wanted to do the right thing and settle down, she would be the one he would wife up.

"The fuck you talking about? What you know about Alanee?"

"Did you forget who you were talking to? I know everything you do and everybody you fuck, so I don't know why you try to keep that shit a secret. Besides, you know I don't give a damn about what you do outside of here as long as you keep it real with me."

"Well, I'm trying to keep it real with this hard on. You can't be answering the door looking like a tasty vanilla treat and not give a nigga some play."

"Sorry, Bak, but as wet as I am right now, I'm gonna have to pass. Maybe next time you wanna hit this, you'll leave ya boy at home because, as long as he's with you, ain't shit poppin off. Besides, my cousin, Jarell, is supposed to be coming through, and I ain't about to have a nigga up in my shit when he gets here."

"Your cousin, huh? You sho that's who's coming? Or you trying to get rid of me, so the next nigga can slide?"

"Your ass don't run shit up in here so miss me with the questioning. I'm single because I ain't about to have no man dictate what I do or who I do it with, and if you wanna keep coming around, you better remember not to question that. Now go ahead on. I got some things to do before my cousin shows up. Oh, yeah, please remember not to bring your tag along next time you come this way."

Trameeka smiled deviously, and before Bak had a chance to say anything else, she slammed the door in his face. She had never just dissed him like that before, so it had him wondering what was really going on. He turned around and walked back to his ride. Something in his gut told him that she wasn't being completely honest. He still couldn't believe that she had brought up Alanee's name. He needed to know where she had heard it at or who she had heard it from. He did his best to keep Alanee sheltered from all the nonsense in his life. Everyone else he fucked with had been messed up individuals, and she seemed to be the only sane thing in his world. He knew that he was wrong for being unfaithful to her, but he still had a few tunnels to explore before his flashlight got turned completely off. Deep down, he truly cared for her, but he just wasn't ready to give her his all.

Bak pulled the half smoked blunt out of the ashtray and lit it. He inhaled the smoke and then drove to Brightman's house without one word. His friend knew him well enough to know that something was seriously off. He didn't want to pry, but he felt like it was his personal duty to make sure his partner was straight.

"Nigga, you mighty quiet. The fuck is up with that?"

Bak blew out a cloud of smoke and answered. "Meeka's ass mentioned Lanee. She speaks about a lot of my bitches, but she never knew about her. I'm just trying to figure out how she linked us together."

"You shoulda known that it would get out one day, and I bet it was Lanee who put it out there. She ain't that high school senior anymore, bruh. She done found her womanhood and probably ready to get out and explore it. That bitch, Erica, you let her hang with got her in places that ain't fit for a female like Lanee, and I'm sure when she's out, she represents you to the fullest. She's only doing what's natural."

Bak knew that it had been fucked up for him to leave Alanee alone so much. He had to predict that she would eventually want to get out and do other things, especially after she'd crept up on his indiscretions. He still remembered the last one as if it were yesterday. One of his other bitches had sent him a text, but he had been asleep, tired from all the good sex that him and Alanee had shared. He had left his cell phone on the kitchen counter, and when it buzzed, she picked it up and checked it - not because she didn't trust him but because she didn't know any better. Reading the text and then seeing the naked flick that was attached had fucked her up, and they hadn't been the same since.

Bak laid the blunt back in the ashtray and thought about Alanee's friend, Erica. He licked his lips every time he was able to steal a glance at her fat camel toe. He believed that she intentionally wore tight pants around him to entice his manhood, and one day, he intended to find out and try to push up on her. He doubted that she would tell Alanee but if she did, fuck it. He would just deny it.

"Brightman, I can't even imagine what would happen if Alanee got loose. She'd be fair game for all those thirsty ass niggas out there, and if it comes to that, I'ma have to kill me a bitch. She belongs to me, and I ain't a mufucka that likes to share, so they better not try me."

"I hear you, bruh, but it's gonna be kinda hard to keep her locked down once she gets a taste of the other side, and I'm sure she's still in her feelings about that shit she found on your phone, not to mention how you stood her up for dinner for another woman. But hey, you already know I got your back, and when it comes to bustin' caps, I'ma ride with you all the way. Just say the word."

The two friends gave each other dap, and then Brightman got out and left Bak to his own thoughts. He was thankful to have a rider on his team like Brightman. He trusted him with his life and felt that he could also trust him with his bitch. Alanee had been out talking a little too much, and he didn't like it, not only because of his other women but because of his enemies too, and he had an abundance of both. He decided that it was time to deal with it, so he put his car in drive and went to go shut Alanee up.

Chapter Four

Jarell knocked on the door with meaning. He was pissed when he found out that Bak had stood Lanee up just so he could try to fuck his cousin. He couldn't be mad at Trameeka because it wasn't her job to change a no-good ass nigga. He smiled when she opened the door because he was always happy to see her. Like him, she was mixed, but people who didn't know mistook her for a white girl. The only thing she inherited from her father's side was the black girl thickness which she carried very well. Her long, silky, black hair was braided back with a few stray curls kissing her face. Trameeka didn't need any makeup, but she loved mascara and lip gloss and wore it even when she wasn't going anywhere.

"Sup, cuz, I hope you got something for me."

"Well, to answer your question, it's the same nigga, but why do you care? What is this girl to you?"

"I met her at the restaurant one night while she was there with her friend, Erica. She, of course, dissed me because she thought I was actually a waiter, and of course, I'm not going to tell her anything different until it's time. She kept mentioning his name, and I remembered you bringing up the same name. I just needed to make sure they're the same before I move in."

"Oh, so you're really interested in this girl?"

"Yeah, I could see some long-term shit with her, but I gotta get this nigga out of the way first."

"He doesn't know it, but he works for Uncle Nahvi."

The sound of his father's name made Jarell perk up. "How long he been working for my pops?"

"Only for about seven months. Before that, he wasn't really bringing in no major flow. His last connect cut him short, so he started to look other places, and that's when he found me. I helped him get his foot in the door, but he thinks it's coming from the Colombians. He's got a two-year-old son, and the bitch that had him tries to suck Bak dry. He needed to find a connect that could bring him a raise, so he could shut the bitch up."

"What exactly does she have to say?"

"She don't know anything about me or Uncle Nahvi so don't worry. She knew every move and every name from his last source. Bak's the type of nigga that likes to brag, but he don't see the drop offs or pickups, so he don't have much to brag about except the money he's making."

"Why is she still breathing? You're not afraid he will end up singing and sharing what he knows with her?"

Trameeka shook her head and pressed her lips together. "He knows if I catch wind of it, he'll never sell another piece of dope in the state. I intrigue him because I hold the power. He just doesn't know how much. And as far as the bitch is concerned, no one has given me the word to handle it, and until she becomes a threat to me or my family, I see no reason to shed blood. I hang on to Bak's ass just so I can keep tabs on her. He's a bitch but fucking with me keeps his mouth shut."

Jarell got quiet and thought about what his next move would be while Trameeka leaned back on the couch and lit a neatly rolled blunt. She knew that he hated it when she got high, but she was grown and controlled her own destiny. She had become a major player in Nahvi's organization. While Jarell turned away from the dope game, she embraced it. No one ever suspected it, so that kept her out of harm's way.

She exhaled and released the smoke from her lungs and sat back up. "You want the nigga out?"

"Out of what?"

"I could get his supply stopped. Might make Alanee pull away."

"Nah, I want Alanee to want to be with me. She only acts materialistic, but I know deep inside she really only wants to be loved and respected. I can give her that, even though she thinks I'm just a waiter in an expensive restaurant."

"When you gonna let her see the truth? If you trying to finesse her, you'll only be able to hide who you are for so long."

"She's already seen the truth. She's just having a hard time believing it."

"I've never seen you act like this over a female before. You really do feel something for her."

"Yeah, cuz. I don't know what it is, but shit feels right when I'm around her. I'm trying to be around her all the time."

Jarell stood, and when Trameeka stood with him, they shared a hug and walked together to her front door. She had never seen her cousin be that invested in a woman before, and if she had to set Bak up to get Alanee from him, she would, but little did she know, he had already fucked himself.

Chapter Five

"Uh uh, bitch. There's something you ain't telling me, and I want in. I know that look, and I got a feeling that Bak ain't the one that gave it to you."

"Whatever, Erica. There ain't shit to tell."

As hard as Alanee tried, she couldn't get Jarell off her mind, and it showed all over her face. She was glad that Bak stood her up because it gave her some time with him. He had made something inside of her shift, and she couldn't lie. It scared the hell outta her. She felt like a bunch of butterflies had been released inside of her stomach. A feeling that no one, not even Bak, could give her. She didn't want to speak too much on it because she hadn't planned on letting it be anything more than what it was. And as hard as she tried to hide it, she had failed because Erica knew her so well.

"You called that fine ass waiter, didn't you?"

"No, I didn't call him. I actually went back to the restaurant and ended up having dinner with him because Bak's sorry ass stood me up."

"What? You mean to tell me that you were supposed to meet Bak at that same restaurant? Girl, you were really trying to rub it in that you had a man. I gotta admit I'm glad he stood you up, and now, your ass better get to talking and don't leave nothing out."

"Erica, I've already told you that there ain't nothing to tell so leave it alone."

"Something else happened with Bak besides that, didn't it? You might as well spit it out because you know my nagging ass ain't gonna shut up until you do, and even if you don't tell me, you know I'll find out another way."

"Okay, damn. After we left the restaurant the other night and I dropped you off, I thought about what you had said about Gina and her son. I just couldn't get it out of my head. Well, Bak told me he had to go out of town on business, which was nothing unusual, but something in my gut told me it was a lie. I decided to drive by Gina's instead of coming back home, and that bastard's car was in her driveway. I was so sick after seeing that, and I came home and cried all night."

"Oh, Lanee, I am so sorry. Why didn't you come get me, so I could be there for you? I tried to tell you, and I don't know why you didn't believe me because I would never bring you no bullshit. I always verify my shit before I talk about it. What kind of friend would I be if I would have kept you in the blind about that? But the real question is what are you going to do about it?"

"I was gonna call his ass out on it and see if he would tell me the truth, but he didn't even show up. I just don't understand why he does me like that. I'm a good girlfriend, and I don't deserve to be lied to and cheated on. That shit just ain't right. Remember when I found those texts and pictures on his phone? Well, he swore that it was the last time, and it would never happen again. My dumb ass really believed him. He made a promise to me, and he broke it, and if I find out that Gina's son is really his, I ain't gonna ever be the same."

Erica comforted her friend but smiled on the inside because she felt like she was one step closer to having M'Baku to herself. She could care less about his multiple women as long as it didn't affect his performance with her. Once she hooked him, she hoped that Alanee would understand but if not, fuck it. Erica felt like it was her time to shine. Alanee had been in the spotlight long enough, and she was tired of her having all the name brand clothes and shoes while she had to walk around in knock offs. That shit had gotten old, and it was time for the tables to turn.

"Now you know that all you're going to do is forgive him like you did before. You shouldn't have took him back after you came up on those texts because you need to know that men don't change. You let them get away with it once, and they'll just continue to do it over and over. You need to leave his ass alone and let those scrubs have him. He needs to be taught a lesson. I mean, Jarell seems like a good enough guy. He just needs to get a better job and get his paper up."

"Oh, he will definitely have to do that, but until I talk to Bak and see what's going on with him and Gina, I can't be hanging out with Jarell. If I did, that would make me just as bad as Bak."

"Speaking of Bak, it sounds like he just pulled up. I think I'm gonna get out of here, so you can handle your business. Don't take too long though because something better might just slip through your hands. Later, bitch."

When Erica opened Alanee's front door to leave, she came face to face with the object of her desire. She looked him up and down and smiled. "What's up, Bak?" she asked as she watched his eyes travel to her print. She pulled his phone from his grasp and programmed her number into it and passed it back. He licked his lips when she walked past him, and she made sure to brush up against his dick, so he would know that she was down for whatever. Bak shook his head and went inside the condo he had put Alanee in. He chose not to stay with her because he enjoyed his freedom too much, but he came and went as he pleased. He felt like he didn't owe her any type of explanation because he was the one who paid the bills. When he allowed her to get a job and pay her own way, that was when she would have some say so and not a second before.

He read her expression before he even got close. "Here we go with the bullshit."

"Yeah, Bak, you can call it what you want but how you doing me is wrong."

"The fuck is you talking about?"

"First of all, you said you were going out of town, but I saw your car parked in Gina's driveway. Then, you were supposed to meet me at the restaurant, and you stood me up. Why, Bak? Did you need some more time with your son or something? I never question you, but do you wanna explain that to me? How the hell do you have a two-year-old son when we've been together for five years?"

Bak scrunched his eyebrows together and ran up on her with an angry look on his face. "First of all, I ain't gotta explain shit to you. I run this mufuckin thing we got going on, and until you start paying some damn bills around here, you ain't got shit else to say."

"Come on, Bak. You have no reason to treat me like this. Don't I deserve some type of respect from you?"

"You deserve just what I give you because I make the rules. Now if you got a problem with that then get your ass out and get a job and take care of your mufuckin self. Ungrateful bitch."

"Ungrateful? How, Bak? You keep me cooped up in this condo and stop by whenever the hell you want to, but you have never thought about how it makes me feel. I've been with you for five years, and it pisses me off that it took me so long to realize what a piece of shit you really are. I can't do this no more, Bak. I just can't do it."

Bak could not believe what he had just heard. He had kept his son with Gina under wraps by putting the kid off on Brightman, but somehow, Alanee had found out the truth. He had never meant to get Gina pregnant, but when the condom took the heat out of his passion, he pulled it off and went raw. The pussy was so good that he couldn't pull out and ended up planting his seeds deep inside of her. He never expected Alanee to find out the truth.

"So, since you can't do it no more, what's your ass still doing here? Pack that shit up and get the hell out."

Alanee was stunned. She expected Bak to regret the things he had done and beg for her forgiveness, but it had backfired. She had given up so much of herself already at his expense and didn't have any more to give, but she also didn't have anywhere to go.

"No, Bak, we can work this out. I didn't mean…"

"I don't give a damn what you meant. Get the hell outta my shit. I'ma teach your ass how to respect a grown man's mind. You should have appreciated a good thing while you had it."

"Bak, come on. You can't be serious. Please tell me you don't mean it. I won't ever mention Gina and her son again. I give you my word. We can work through this. I was speaking out of hurt. That's all."

Alanee reached out to grab his hand, but he pulled it back and shook his head. He hated a disobedient woman, especially one he had invested so much time and money on.

"Your momma should have taught you not to question a man, but since she obviously didn't, you gonna have to pay for that. I want your ass outta here before I get back and don't take anything you didn't pay for because my other bitch might need it." Bak turned to leave, but before he walked out, he had one more thing to say. "And don't let me find out you ran to anotha nigga because once you mine, you always mine, even when you ain't with me."

On his way out, he noticed her Fendi bag as it hung on a hook by the door. He opened it and reached inside, so he could retrieve her keys. She couldn't believe he had the audacity to take everything she had, including her transportation.

"No, Bak, how do you expect me to get around without my car?"

"Walk yo' ass to the bus stop. I'm out."

Alanee fell to her knees in tears because she had no clue what she was going to do. She had bypassed college, so she could be with him. He told her that if she went off to school, she would lose out on her chance to be with him. How could he do her so dirty after all they had been through together?

She thought about where she would go and knew that her options were limited. Her parents had disowned her when she chose a street nigga over her education so calling them was not going to happen. There was no way in hell she'd stay with Erica and her mother because the neighborhood alone gave her the creeps. True enough, she went through there to pick Erica up and drop her off, but she never cut off her engine. Alanee liked hood niggas, but she never wanted to live the hood lifestyle. While she was contemplating on what to do, another thought crossed her mind. She dried her eyes, sucked in her emotions, and dialed a number she already knew by heart.

Chapter Six

The ringing of Jarell's cell phone brought him out of the deep slumber he had fallen into. He had been exhausted from the long hours he had been putting in at the restaurant, but there was no one else he could depend on to do the job. He was grateful to be able to finally take a break because it was one he desperately needed. There were few people he fucked with and even fewer that had his number. He knew if someone was calling him that late, it had to be important, so he couldn't just lie there and ignore it.

He slowly reached over and picked his phone up off the nightstand. He looked at the number but didn't recognize it but decided to answer it anyway. "Yeah, the fuck is calling me this late?"

The sound of Alanee's voice that came from the other end caused him to sit up and pay close attention. He wanted to be fully alert, so he didn't miss one syllable that came from her lips. She was the last person he expected, but he was glad to hear from her.

"Jarell, I know it's late, and I'm sorry to disturb you, but I didn't have anyone else I could call."

"Lanee, what's going on? Are you okay? You sound like something is wrong."

"It's worse than wrong. Me and Bak got into it really bad, and he told me I had to leave. He wouldn't let me take anything with me that I didn't bring. He even took my car keys and phone. I didn't know what else to do. Jarell, I know I haven't been very nice to you, but I really need you right now. Could you please come pick me up? I've never really been out here by myself before, so I'm a little weary."

"I'ma come get you. Just tell me where you at."

She told Jarell her location and hung up. He could hear the fear in her voice, and it caused his nose to flare in anger. He quickly went into the bathroom and washed away the evidence of sleep from his eyes. After he brushed his perfect, white teeth, he pulled on a wife beater and slid on a light jacket that matched the pair of sweatpants he had pulled up over his boxer briefs. After he slid on a pair of Jordans, he grabbed his keys and was out the door. His E class Mercedes sitting on deep dish 22s started with ease as always.

As soon as the engine roared to life, the smooth melodic voice of Jaheim filled the air. "You can have anything I got, all of me right on the spot, da, da da da, da da da, da da, da da da da. You can have anything I own, work my fingers all the way to the bone, da da da, da da da, da da da, da da." No matter how old the song became, it still put him in a zone, and he could listen to it over and over. He hoped that Alanee would end up being the woman he could give anything to. Only time would give him his answer.

Even with a broken heart, Alanee's beauty never ceased. Jarell could see the pain in her eyes every time he looked into them, and he knew that night would be no different. All he wanted to do was mend her heart back together, but she had to be willing to let him. What kind of man could hurt something so precious and fragile? He knew that she wouldn't expect him to pull up in a Benz, and when he drove up beside her and rolled down the window, he smiled as if nothing was off.

"You look like you seen a ghost."

"Uh, no. I just... I wasn't expecting you to pull up in... well, you know, a Mercedes."

"Oh, yeah. That's right. Ain't no way a waiter could afford to drive around in such luxury, huh?"

She held her head low in embarrassment. "Look, I'm really not a materialistic woman. I'm just used to certain things after being with Bak for so long. I wasn't trying to offend you. God, I am so ashamed."

"Na, Ma, you ain't gotta be ashamed. Just don't judge a book by its cover. Open that bitch up and read it first because you just might like the story inside. Now, let me get you out of here."

Jarell put his arm around her and led her to the passenger side of the vehicle. She looked almost confused when he opened up the car door for her. He knew it wasn't a courtesy that the last nigga extended. Growing up, his father may have taught him how to be a thug, but he also taught him how to be a gentleman when it came to the ladies. Nahvi told him that an inconsiderate man had no place on Earth, and no matter how a woman looked or acted, she was still a queen and should always be treated as such.

Jarell followed his father's advice in the past, but it was never appreciated. The few women he had dated all wanted the same thing, money and status. None had been worthy of the heart Jarell held inside his chest, so he never gave it to any of them. However, Alanee was already strong arming a piece of it.

Jarell broke the silence that had filled the inside of the car and brought Alanee out of her thoughts.

"You got somewhere you want me to take you, or we just gonna ride around town for a while?"

"Trying to get rid of me so soon?"

"I'm actually trying to do the opposite, but you keep playing hard to get. You act like you can't give an ole waiter a chance."

"Okay, you got me. I deserved that. Are you gonna ever let that go?"

"Sure, I can let it go but what I can't let go is you."

"How can you say that when you don't even have me yet, and there's no guarantees you'll get me?"

Jarell pulled into the parking garage of the massive building he lived in and shut the engine off. He turned to Alanee and ran a finger over her perfect pouty lips. "I always get what I want, and once you get to know me, you'll find that out for yourself."

Jarell's touch made Alanee speechless, and she enjoyed the feeling it had given her. She didn't want to seem easy, and she knew that if she didn't distance herself from him, she could very well fall in unknown territory. She also knew that she wouldn't be able to fight with what her heart was telling her. She was still in deep thought and didn't realize he had gotten out until the passenger side door opened. A slight breeze entered the car and brought her back to the real world.

"Where are we at?"

"Well, I figured since you didn't have anyone else to call, that meant you also didn't have anywhere else to stay. So, I guess you just gonna have to chill at my place until you can figure the whole thing out."

Alanee grabbed the small backpack she had carried. It wasn't much, but it would be enough until she could get a job and get on her feet. She had never held a job before, but she would do her best to find one.

The elevator ride up felt like it took forever to get to its destination, and when she heard the ding, it caused her to flinch. Jarell took notice and wondered just how much damage Bak had really done.

"It's aiight, Ma. You safe with me." And for some reason, she believed him.

Jarell opened the door of the penthouse and let Alanee walk in first. She couldn't believe her eyes after she saw the extravagant layout. She wondered how he was able to afford the light gray Ben Soleimani sectional. She figured that somewhere along the way, she had misjudged him. She felt his presence behind her and turned around to face him. She wanted to ask him questions that she was sure he didn't want to answer, but before she could get a word out, his lips found hers, and all train of thought had been interrupted. When their lips finally separated, Jarell walked away and left her standing there, hoping she could find her composure.

Alanee smiled deep inside, but she wasn't about to let him get away with the stolen kiss that easily. She refused to come off as someone he could try like that. They barely knew each other, so he had no right. She stormed into the open kitchen area, but once she got there and faced him, the words would not come out. Her heart sped as she watched him stand in front of the stove and prepare some food in only a pair of Columbia boxer briefs. She first noticed the numerous tattoos that adorned his toned physique. They glowed brightly against his light skin. She tried to follow a web that started behind his left ear and traveled around and down his spine, only to continue down the waist of his briefs. She couldn't be sure where it ended, but she could almost guess its destination.

She noticed the black widow that looked so real that she swore that it had moved and began to crawl down his skin. She had the sudden urge to flick it off of him but was too afraid it would bite her. She felt like she had committed a crime once he turned to face her, and her eyes went straight to the bulge in the fabric that kissed his skin. She swallowed so hard that she could have sworn he heard her.

He followed her eyes down and smiled. "You hungry?"

The question caught her off guard. "What did you say?"

"I asked if you was hungry. If you sit down and put something on your stomach, it will help you sleep so much better."

Her mind thought about something else that would help her sleep, but she knew she had to be modest about the situation. "I didn't know you could cook. You just don't seem like the type."

"I didn't know there was a certain type you had to be to put out a good meal."

"I didn't… I don't know. You seem like the fast food, snack eating, Sunday at Momma's type."

Jarell couldn't help but laugh because she had him pegged all wrong. If she was surprised that he could cook, he couldn't wait til she found out other things about him.

"My momma taught me how to cook as I was growing up. She didn't want me to ever have to be dependent on a woman for anything, so she taught me the skills I needed to be independent. She also did it just in case I met and fell in love with a woman who couldn't cook."

"A woman like me? Well, other than the falling in love part."

"Don't sell yourself or my feelings short and don't tell me that you don't know how to throw down in the kitchen. You gotta be kidding me."

"No, I've never had a reason to. Bak never stuck around long enough to eat anything but me, and apparently, I wasn't enough to fill him up."

"I don't understand how any nigga would prefer take out over a home cooked meal, especially something so delicately made."

Alanee had the feeling that he wasn't talking about real food, and it caused her to blush. She felt like a high school senior all over again, and it made her think of Bak. She remembered how he had finessed her at the beginning of their relationship, only to change things up as time passed. He hadn't respected her in a long time, and she looked over it constantly. She knew that she was wrong for running to Jarell, but she just couldn't understand why it felt so right.

"Do you think your boss would give me a job?"

"What? You? A waitress? After all the shit you gave me about being a waiter? Now that's funny."

"Come on. I'm being serious. I don't have any other options. I have to figure out something so that I can get back on my feet. I was so used to Bak taking care of me, so it's all going to feel strange, but I don't have another choice. You got any brilliant ideas?"

"Ya know, if you was mine, you would never have to worry about all that. I would enjoy taking care of you. But since you're not, I'll think about putting in a word with the boss for you."

"Thanks. I appreciate that, and I'm not going to impose on your space, so in the morning, I'll call Erica and see if her mom has room for one more."

"Yeah, about your friend. You shouldn't trust her. I know a snake when I see one, and you don't have to call anybody because you're more than welcome to stay here for as long as you need."

"I'll take heed to your warning, but Erica has been my best friend since high school, and we've never had any trust issues. She's like a sister to me, so don't worry about her, and I do appreciate the offer for me to stay here, but I don't want to be here when one of your women comes knocking, so I'm going to pass on that one."

"My woman, huh? That's something you don't have to worry your pretty little head about. There's only one I want and if I can't have her, then I don't want nobody."

Alanee knew that he was talking about her, but instead of responding, she shoved a forkful of scrambled eggs in her mouth. She admired his bluntness, but she had to make sure he wasn't just another smooth talker. She also had to make sure that she was completely done with Bak.

Jarell sat there and watched her eat, but when he realized that he was making her nervous, he got up. "I'm gonna go get the guest bedroom ready for you unless you're afraid to sleep alone."

"No, I think I can manage sleeping by myself. That's another thing I'm used to doing, but if I happen to see any monsters in the closet, I'll make sure to call you, so you can rescue me."

"To be honest, I think I already have."

Jarell walked off and left Alanee to think about what he'd said. He was elated that she called him, but how long could he get her to stay? He knew that he might actually have to eliminate Bak, and he knew just who to go to so he could put his plan in play.

Chapter Seven

Bak leaned back on the plush sofa and lit the freshly rolled blunt. He had never smoked Kush in the condo before, not because he couldn't but because he was too afraid that Alanee would blow his high. He hated to waste good weed, so he always made sure he waited to get his fix until after he spent time with her. The condo seemed empty without her presence but fuck it. He wasn't about to sulk over a bitch. He would just find a new one to replace her, one that would sit back and keep her nose where it belonged. He couldn't stand to be questioned because he was grown and felt like he didn't owe anyone an explanation for anything he did.

When he retreated to the condo, it told his whole crew that he didn't want to be fucked with. He felt like he didn't have to worry about a nigga running up on him while he was there either. He appreciated the fact that he had somewhere he could go and relax and gain a peace of mind.

As soon as he topped off the blunt, he sat back up and opened the duffel bag that sat on the floor beside his Nike tennis shoes. He smiled at the contents and then began to empty it. He thought about how good life had been to him as he stacked the bundles of money one on top of the other. Staring at all the hard made Benjamins made his dick hard. He had always fantasized about fucking a bitch on top of a bed that was covered in nothing but green bills. He thought about who he could call to make his fantasy come true, and as soon as he pulled his cell phone out to dial a honey up, he heard the doorbell ring.

Since he had not been expecting anybody, he took caution and pulled his four five out from under the cushion of the couch. He kinda hoped that it was Alanee coming back to beg for forgiveness, but when he opened the door, he had a shocking surprise.

"What's going on, Bak? Is Alanee here?"

He licked his lips as he looked Erica up and down. He could tell she didn't have on a bra because her fat, perky nipples poked out like thorns on a rose stem. Her pants were so tight it looked like her pussy was eating the fabric.

"Nah, Lanee ain't here."

Erica stepped a little closer to him, just to see if he would pull back, "Is she gonna be back soon?"

"Lanee ain't coming back. A nigga like me ain't got time for all those damn questions. I need me a bitch that knows how to shut her mouth and open them thighs to keep a nigga on his toes. You know a bitch that can do that for me?"

"You staring that bitch in the face right now."

"You gon' flip on ya girl like that? Ain't y'all got some kind of friendship code about things like that?"

"Nah, I ain't never heard of no code like that. Besides, I'm sure she's with that waiter she met and ain't thinking about my ass."

"Waiter? The hell is you talking about, Erica?"

"Nothing important, Bak. I'm probably just speaking nonsense because when we was at the restaurant, she did diss his ass. My bad. I shouldn't have even said anything."

Bak knew that she was hiding something because she acted like she knew more than she was saying. He needed to know just who Erica had been talking about, and he knew just what to give her to make her sing. He opened the front door wider and stepped to the side, so she could walk past him.

"Fuck Alanee and whatever nigga she kicking it with. I'm trying to lay in something warm on top of all that money I got stacked up."

"Oh, yeah, I got something real warm. Actually, I got something to make you sweat."

Erica walked up to him and pulled his bottom lip into her mouth, but Bak wasn't trying to do all that kissing. His dick was hard, and he was ready for some action. He pushed her back from him lightly and nodded toward the couch. She looked and saw all the money that was stacked up on the table and then walked over to it. Without even asking, she picked up four stacks and popped the band that was on them. When she spread it out on the sofa and then stripped, Bak smiled.

He walked over to the couch and let her strip off his clothes. As soon as he sat down, she took him in her mouth and changed the course of her relationship with Alanee forever.

Bak fucked Erica in every position he could get her in, and then, the two smoked a blunt together. He didn't know why he hadn't got with her before then because she seemed like a down bitch. He liked the fact that he could sit back, fuck, and enjoy his high without any nagging or complaining. The fact that she could ride him the way he liked pleased him even more; however, the best part of it all was when she spread her legs and touched her own womanhood. He had tried many nights to get Alanee to put on a show for him, but she just wouldn't cooperate. That freaky shit had him in a zone that he had longed to travel, but he also had to remember that she did it all behind Alanee's back, someone he thought she considered a friend. So, to Bak, that meant she would go behind his back too. He knew he couldn't trust her, so he would be careful.

Between the weed and good pussy, Bak was spent. He was glad that he didn't have any business to deal with, and he could afford to take a night off from the block. He looked over and saw Erica was asleep, so he got up and went to the bathroom, so he could take a long, hot, much needed shower. He turned on the water and got in and stood under the flowing waterfall. He was so into the feeling that he didn't even hear the doorbell.

Erica thought she was hearing things until she heard it again. She opened her eyes slowly and looked around, and all she saw was hundred-dollar bills scattered everywhere. Her pussy throbbed from the beating Bak had put on it, and she smiled at the thought of finally getting what she wanted. When she heard the doorbell again, she looked around for Bak but didn't see him. She knew he couldn't have gone far because there was no way he would leave her alone with all that money. She decided to answer the door, but instead of putting on her own clothes, she picked up Bak's Sean John jersey and covered her nakedness.

"I'm coming. Damn. Hold on."

Erica didn't bother to look through the peephole but instead opened the door without another thought. as if she was in her own house. She almost pissed on herself when she saw who was on the other side.

"Alanee. Oh, my God. What are you doing here?"

"Erica, why are you here? And why do you have on Bak's jersey? Bitch, what the hell is going on?"

About that time, Bak walked out of the bathroom with his dick freely swinging, as if he didn't have a care in the world. When he noticed Erica wasn't on the couch where he'd left her, he went in search of her, but he didn't have to go very far.

"You bastard. I can't believe you would do this to me."

When he saw Erica at the door and Alanee standing in front of her, he didn't know what to do. He didn't want to come between the two of them, but he was weakened by the need for a nut. He had cheated on Alanee many times, but he had never hit so close to home.

"Aye, Lanee, this shit wasn't supposed to happen like this."

"Oh, yeah, well, how was it supposed to happen, Bak? How could you and Erica do this to me?"

Erica wasn't about to listen to a pity party, so she spoke her peace and didn't give a damn who liked it or not. "You know what, Lanee? You shoulda known that something like this would eventually happen. But I guess you probably never felt like Bak would fuck with me. So, what, I may not be as thick or even as pretty as you, but bitch, I know how to sit back and play my fucking position. Something you never could do."

"Your position? Bitch, you don't have a position."

"I must have something since I'm the one standing here with his shirt on and with a hundred-dollar bill stuck to my ass. You said you was sick of his shit anyway, so now you don't have to worry about him anymore. You should be grateful that I took him off your hands."

Alanee looked from Erica to Bak, and her heart broke even more. He had done her wrong so many times, but she could forgive all of those misdeeds. However, there was no way she could overlook his indiscretion with someone she considered to be her friend. Alanee had never been the type to fight, but she had the sudden urge to want to bust Erica in her mouth, but she just wasn't worth it.

"I knew you were always jealous, but you didn't want to admit it. You've slithered under me all these years, and I can't even believe that I didn't see it! Jarell was right. He told me I shouldn't trust you, but I told him that he was wrong."

"Ah, suck it up, Lanee. We done been through a lot of shit. I know we can work this out like we have everything else. Girl, I know you ain't gonna let a community dick come between us."

"No, Erica, we can't come back from this. I hope you enjoy getting treated like shit because if you think he's going to do right by you then you are sadly mistaken."

Alanee felt as if the tears would fall and betray her, but she managed to keep her composure. She refused to let Bak and Erica see the effects of what they'd done to her. She didn't need either one of them. She looked at Bak one more time and then turned around to leave. She couldn't stand to be in their presence anymore, but before she walked out the door, she had one more thing to say.

"Both of you will get what you deserve. You can mark my words on that."

The two of them laughed at her comment, but neither one of them could have imagined just how much karma would ultimately slap them right in the face.

Chapter Eight

Alanee could have sworn that working alongside of Jarell at the restaurant would help ease her mind of all the bullshit and drama going on in her life. She still found it hard to believe that Erica had stabbed her so deep in the spine. She was supposed to be her best friend, and even though she didn't expect anything less from Bak, she just wished that he would have done it with someone else.

She had only been apart from Bak for a short minute, but she thought that he would have called and apologized, but then she remembered that she didn't even have a phone for him to call. The day she had gone to try and get it was the day that she'd caught him with Erica, and she left without another thought of why she'd gone there in the first place. Alanee just couldn't believe that he was sticking dick to someone who was like a sister to her. She had never felt so disrespected in her life. She thought she had noticed the signs when Erica would come around, and Bak would be there. Erica's body language spoke volumes along with the skimpy shirts and tight jeans, but Alanee chose to brush it off. They had been through the mud together and always came out with their friendship still intact, but Alanee knew there was no way they would recover from what had taken place.

"You just gon' stand there and daydream, or you gonna give a nigga a table, so he can eat?"

The sound of Bak's voice caused chills to climb up her spine. She couldn't believe that he had the audacity to show his face anywhere that she was at. She wasn't sure what to expect from him, so she decided to just act normal.

"Are you going to be dining alone tonight?"

"Hell nah. My bitch will be joining me so make sure you sit us somewhere private and make sure I'll be able to watch you. Ain't no telling what your ass might do."

"Look, Bak, I haven't even thought about you or Erica for that matter. I ain't trying to cause y'all no trouble, and even though y'all didn't give a damn about my feelings, I just want to be left alone. You two deserve each other but please don't be coming up in here and rubbing it in my face. I'm really trying to move on and do something better for myself. Please don't jeopardize what I've accomplished."

Before Bak could say anything else, Erica walked up and smiled at Alanee. It took all of her willpower not to reach out and slap the smile off of Erica's face. After all that she had done to her, Alanee found the strength to give her back a fake smile and stated, "Follow me. I have the perfect table for y'all."

When they got to the table, Bak reached and pulled out Erica's chair and then sat down opposite of her. Erica looked up at her ex-friend and said something Alanee didn't expect. "Lanee, I really am sorry that things turned out this way, and I just hope that we can move past this and salvage our friendship. We always swore that we would never let a nigga come between us, so we can't let this move us. You kept saying that you was tired of his ass, so I did you a favor and took him off your hands. You should be grateful."

"Grateful? No, bitch, I'll tell you what I'm grateful for, and that's the fact that your true colors have finally shown. You truly deserve a man like Bak, and if you think he's going to treat you any better than he did me, then you are sadly mistaken. Bak is a piece of shit, and a piece of shit never loses its smell."

"Aw, that's really cute. Are you feeling some type of way about this? Well, you shouldn't because you gonna be alright, girl. Ain't you got that waiter that works here? At least now y'all are on the same level."

"You bitch. I should…"

Bak stood up from his seat and stepped in front of Alanee. Him being that close to her used to make her heart speed up, but that feeling was long gone. She held nothing but disgust for him, and he made her skin crawl, and all she wanted was for him to back away from her.

"Aiight, this shit has gone on long enough. I'm sick of hearing y'all go at each other, so y'all need to either kiss and make up or fight that shit out because I'm getting real bored. I'm also hungry so do your damn job and go get me some fuckin' food."

Alanee couldn't even find the words to say to him. After all that she had been through with him, and all that she had given up for him, he never could appreciate her. He had tried to justify it all by spoiling her with money and nice things, but none of it could have ever been enough. She had passed up going to college and being cut off by her parents, just to give him the time of day. All she ever really wanted in return was his love, but she had never been worthy of it. She sucked in a deep breath, looked in his eyes one last time, and then walked away.

On the way back to the kitchen, she bumped into Jarell. He could tell that something was wrong with her, so when she tried to get past him, he pulled her into his arms and stopped her.

"Why you lookin like that, Ma? Didn't I tell you to always hold that pretty head up? Come on. Shit can't be that bad. You still got me."

"I'm cool, Jarell, but you're going to have to get someone else to wait my section because I'm telling you now if I go back out there, I'm putting a bitch in the hospital."

Jarell scrunched his eyebrows together and then looked around the corner, so he could see just what had Alanee so upset. He couldn't believe that Bak had the nerve to show up there with Erica. He had told Alanee that the bitch was a snake, but she had finally found out for herself.

"Look, how 'bout you go take a break, and I'll handle that for you? I'll let you know when they leave."

"Are you sure, Jarell? It's not right for me to send you out into my drama. Why don't you let someone else handle it?"

"What? You ain't figured out yet that I want to be in it? I got this so go on and chill out."

"Thanks."

She puckered up her lips and then tiptoed, so she could give him a kiss on the cheek, but Jarell turned his head and caused their lips to meet instead. Alanee became lost in the magic of his tongue, and when she closed her eyes, all her troubles seemed to disappear. When their kiss broke and Jarell pulled back, she continued to stand there with her eyes closed. When she heard Jarell laugh, she opened them and looked into his handsome face. She had never seen a man so perfectly made, but there he was, in front of her, and all she could do was stare.

"I could stand here all night and do this with you, but I gotta go handle that nigga first. Hold that thought though because we ain't done."

Jarell walked away and left her in a daze. Her lips throbbed from the passion they had shared. She swore that after Bak broke her heart, she would never give it to another man, but Jarell was making it hard to keep her word. She had tried her best to fight how she felt, but she had grown tired of fighting. She decided that she was going to give him the chance he had been asking for, one that he had truly earned. Him being a waiter no longer mattered to her. She admired his hardworking persona. She figured it had taken him a long time to be able to afford the Benz and penthouse suite. She had seen plenty of broke niggas living in luxury and driving a nice ride, just to show off. Those same niggas couldn't even afford a steak dinner from Ruth's Chris. However, those things seemed to mean less and less as the days went by. Bak had spoiled her for so long, and at the end of the day, it really didn't mean shit. She didn't care what Jarell could or couldn't afford to do for her because, at the end of the day, her love didn't cost a thing.

Jarell licked the cherry flavor that Alanee had left behind off of his lips and walked up to the table that Bak and Erica sat at. Bak had no clue who he was, but Erica did, and still, she had read him wrong. She thought that since she was fucking Bak that she was above everyone else, but little did she know, Jarell had the connections to bring her back down to size.

"I apologize for the sudden change in waitstaff, but Miss Travis had to tend to something else. I'm here to take her place and am more than happy to take your order."

Erica let out a slight laugh and placed her hand over Bak's. "Baby, that's Jarell, the little waiter that has a thing for Lanee."

"Oh, yeah. This the nigga that's been trying to get with my bitch?"

The comment threw Erica off because she was his bitch now. She decided to say something to him about it after Jarell left to get their food, but he acted like the food they wanted no longer mattered. "I don't know what bitch you're referring to, but the only one I see is sitting in front of you. Does Trameeka know that you been taking out the trash?"

Bak stood and came face to face with Jarell. "The fuck you know about Trameeka, nigga?"

Erica stood quickly and placed her freshly manicured hands on her hips. She knew about most of Bak's other conquests, but she had never heard that name before. "Who in the hell is Trameeka?"

"Bitch, sit yo' ass down and don't ever question me about shit. I'm the only one allowed to ask questions."

"Nigga, fuck you. I'm outta here."

Erica stormed away and thought that Bak would come behind her to try and stop her, but little did she know, he had grown sick of her already. She wasn't the type of chick he could see himself with long term anyway. All she wanted to do was fuck and spend his cash, but the pussy wasn't all that he'd expected, so he got bored with it quickly. The only reason he had taken her out to eat that night was so that he could end things between them. He had also started to miss Alanee, and that was why he had chosen the restaurant she worked at. He didn't know that she'd already had another nigga in her ass, but he was certain she'd choose him over a broke ass waiter.

"Now, nigga, answer my question. The fuck you know about Trameeka?"

Jarell smiled because a nigga like Bak didn't put no fear in his heart. He talked a big game, but at the end of the day, his ass had to get the next man to pull his trigger.

"Why don't you ask her yourself? Go head and ride on over there. Make sure you tell her Jarell sent you. Bitch ass nigga. And stay the hell away from anywhere that Alanee is at. She don't need your bullshit anymore. That's the only warning you gonna get."

Bak didn't know what to say because he didn't know anything about Jarell. Trameeka fucked with very few people so for him to know her meant that he was somebody. Bak just didn't know who, and he wasn't about to fuck up what he had going on with her.

"I will ask her, my nigga, and as far as Alanee goes, she gon' always need me. She used to the good life, and a nine to five mufucka ain't gonna give her that. I'ma let you chill for now, but I'll be back. Tell Lanee to be ready when I do."

Bak shoulder bumped Jarell as he walked away, and no sooner than he was gone, Alanee appeared from around the corner.

"I'm sorry, Jarell. I knew I shouldn't have pulled you into this."

"You ain't pull me into anything I didn't want to be in, and you ain't gotta worry about me. I can handle my own. I was born for shit like that. Now stop worrying and let's get out of here."

"Um, I can't leave right now. I still have a couple of hours left before my shift is over."

"Oh, yeah? Well, what if I told you that I'm in real good with the boss, and I've already talked to him?"

"Well, okay then but can I ask a question?"

"Go head, Ma, whatever you want."

"I'm just curious why I have never met the boss. I mean, how can someone I've never met feel right about giving me a job?"

"Let's just say that he took my word for it, and I can guarantee you that my word is bond. Now come on. I'm ready to go to the crib and chill."

Alanee shrugged her shoulders and took off her apron. She didn't want to say anything, but her feet were killing her. She wished that she would have chosen an office job somewhere instead, but she was so desperate that she took the first thing she could. She couldn't wait to get back to Jarell's place, so she could relax her feet.

Jarell drove slowly under the streetlights because he liked the fact that they gave him quick snapshots of Alanee's beauty. He turned his head to the right and stole a glance at her every chance he got. Her eyes were closed, but he felt like she could feel him watch her. She seemed to be at peace, even with all the chaos that was going on in her life. Jarell was glad that he could make her feel that way. He didn't give a damn about all her drama because he felt like she was worth anything he had to go through. He felt connected to her and was sure that she felt the same.

He pulled into the parking garage and parked. He brushed a finger over her lips, and it caused her to stir. She turned her head and smiled.

"Wake up, sleepy head."

"Yeah, I'm up, but I am so ready to go back to sleep. I'm so exhausted."

"Well, let's go up because I think I have something that will relax you and help you sleep even better."

Alanee raised an eyebrow but liked the sound of what he had said. She wasn't sure what he had in mind, but honestly, she was down for whatever.

As soon as they walked in the penthouse, Alanee sat on the couch and pulled her tennis shoes off. She swore that there had to be something more comfortable for her to work in, and she was determined to find it. She decided that she would also look for a small efficient apartment because she was sure she was imposing on Jarell's space. She began to rub her own feet when she heard J. Valentine's voice fill the room. "You ain't gotta tell me lies. Girl, lift your numbers high. Even if I know, I'm man enough to put that aside. All my boys gon' trip cause this ain't what I do. I don't give a damn. Girl, you're way too much to lose."

She had been singing along to the words when Jarell walked in the living room. She wasn't embarrassed though because for some reason, she had never felt more comfortable in her life. She watched him as he walked over to the couch and sat down beside her. Without asking, he grabbed her legs and pulled them onto his lap. Her mind told her to stop him, but her heart wouldn't let her. He began to rub her feet, something that threw her completely off guard. Bak had never catered to her needs in that way. As a matter of fact, he never paid enough attention to even notice when something was wrong with her.

"I ran you a nice, hot, bubble bath, so you can soak these here dogs in 'em."

"Yeah, they barking loud, ain't they?"

The two shared a laugh and then, just as quickly, got quiet. Jarell put one leg on each side of him and crawled between them to get closer, and when Alanee met him halfway, he knew anything that happened between them that night would change his place in her life forever. She was completely thrown off when he broke their kiss.

"What's wrong, Jarell? Why did you stop kissing me?"

"Don't worry. I ain't done with you, but this isn't where I want this to happen. The fuck I look like making love to you on a couch?"

"It doesn't matter to me where it happens at, but you can't just make a girl wet and leave her hanging."

"Oh, you wet, baby?"

"Drippin."

"Then I guess that means a nigga is doing everything right, but it's gon' take more than this little ole couch. I need room to work my magic."

Alanee smiled at the thought but little did he know that his magic had already worked on her. He had her wetter than she had ever been, and she wanted him inside of her. He stood and then bent down and picked her up. She may have been thick in all the right places, but she was light as a feather. When he got her to the bedroom, he put her down and wanted to make sure that she was okay with what was about to go down.

"You sure you cool with this, Ma? Cause ain't gonna be no turning back. That nigga come for you, I'ma push his wig backwards."

Alanee was shocked at what Jarell said because he seemed like one of those square ass niggas she had avoided for so long, but maybe she missed something along the way. She loved that roughneck gangsta shit, and it only turned her on even more.

"Yeah, Jarell, I'm cool. I want this just as bad as you do."

"Aiight then, but remember you asked for it."

Jarell slowly undressed her, and with each piece of clothing he removed, he ran his tongue down the flesh that had been exposed. Her body was as perfect as he thought it would be. Her breasts were just big enough to fill his hands, and as soon as he ran a thumb over her nipple, it stood and gave him all its attention. He couldn't help but to pull one into his mouth.

"Mmm, Jarell."

Her moans told him everything he needed to know, so he didn't even bother to ask how it felt. Once he let her nipple go, he smiled, and she understood exactly what it meant. She got on the bed and laid back, so she could give him a full view of what now belonged to him. Her diamond belly ring shimmered in the dimly lit room and gave her toned stomach even more definition.

She was fully exposed but felt no shame, and as she watched him pull off his t-shirt, she thought about what Erica had told her. When he pulled a four five from the back waist of his jeans, she didn't want to spoil the mood and ask him why he carried it. so instead, she spread her legs and ran her hand down to her womanhood. The sounds of *Slave* by Jaheim played in the background. "This ain't the part we fall in love. This is the part we kiss and fuck. Do all the things we said we'd never do."

The song was perfect, except for the part about falling in love because Alanee could already feel herself doing just that. She had never felt anything else like it in her life, and she was certain that the feeling wasn't one sided, the way that Bak had been. However, any worries she may have had disappeared as soon as Jarell entered her. He was bigger than she had expected, but she welcomed every inch of him. She rotated her hips, and together, they fell into a rhythm that even Jaheim couldn't match.

"Oh, Jarell. Damn, you feel so good inside of me. Yes, baby. Please don't ever stop. I want all of this dick."

Jarell heard her request and lifted her legs over his shoulders, so he could go deep. He was lost in her wetness and knew that he wouldn't be able to pull out when it was time but fuck it because there was no one else he could think of that he'd rather share that part with. She had him, and he felt like she knew it. She was his Cinderella, and he would cherish her forever.

His father told him that when he found the one, he would feel it all in his chest. His heart gave him the only sign he needed to realize that he would never let Alanee go. He didn't give a damn who or what tried to stand in his way. She was his, and everyone was about to know it.

Chapter Nine

Alanee didn't see him walk in, but she could feel the power of his presence, and it caused her to look up and take notice. She could tell that no matter what room he walked into, he demanded respect, so much that even his enemies couldn't deny him. He was tall, at least six foot two, and slim. The hints of gray in his deep Caesar waves told her that he was wise in years, and the mere thought of approaching him made her nervous, but she couldn't just let him stand there.

She began to walk toward him slowly. She felt like she had seen him somewhere before, but she just couldn't place him. She could smell money seeping through his pores and knew that he was a boss. At one point in his life, he had been a street nigga, but from the looks of him, she was sure that he was retired. She could almost bet money on it. Alanee had seldom been wrong when she read someone, and that thought brought Erica to her mind. The one person she had trusted the most was the one who betrayed her. She wasn't sure if she'd ever be able to trust another, and she damn sure wasn't thinking about forgiveness.

"Good evening, sir. Will you be dining alone tonight?"

As soon as he heard her voice, he turned around and acknowledged her. "As a matter of fact, Alanee, my wife will be joining me."

She wondered how he knew her name because she never wore her name tag. She wanted to ask him, but before she had a chance to, a beautiful white woman walked up and linked her arm with his. She looked well taken care of and well loved. Alanee began to feel a little envious of her because she wanted someone to love her in that same way. She had thought that she found the love she had been looking for when she met Bak, but his kind of love had been poison and slowly drained the air from her lungs. There had been no excuse for what he'd done, but his sin against her pushed her straight to Jarell. She wondered if what her and Jarell had started could possibly turn into what the couple in front of her had. She wanted to ask them what their secret was, but before she could get a word out, Jarell walked up.

"Lanee, I see you've met my parents."

His smile alone told of the admiration and love he held for the couple, and it caused her to miss her own parents. She hoped that one day she'd get the nerve to call them and ask for their forgiveness. She wasn't sure how they'd respond, but it was worth a try.

"Oh, my gosh, I thought he looked like someone I knew. That explains how he knew my name."

"I think I might have mentioned you a time or two."

Ashley raised her brows and then told Alanee the truth. "A time or two? Sweetie, your name has been in every conversation my son and I have had, and I'll let you in on a little secret. We talk every day."

Alanee blushed because the thought of Jarell talking about her to his parents said a lot, and it brought a smile to her face. She knew then that she had found the real thing.

"I'm really flattered that you would mention me to your parents. You really know how to make me feel special."

Jarell bent and kissed her forehead. "You are special, and I'ma spend forever showing you just how much you mean to me."

Janahvi watched the exchange between his son and Alanee closely. It reminded him so much of when he first met Ashley. He knew that she would be it for him. True enough, he had fucked up a time or two, but Ashley rode the wave with him, and their bond still remained strong. He knew that she looked forward to the day that he would exit the game completely, but the streets had been in his blood since he was a jit, and he couldn't imagine leaving it for good. When Meek died, he had stepped back for a minute, but it kept calling him to come back, and eventually, he answered.

When Jarell was growing up, Janahvi swore that he could see the thug mentality playing in his mind, but Ashley begged him not to lead their son to that kind of life. The couple decided to give him a taste of both worlds and then let him make his own choices about his future. Jarell took to the gun like a natural born killer and also embraced the street knowledge his father fed him, but the dope game was not his thing. He saw no need in putting more poison out in the streets to his people. He didn't knock whoever chose to live that way, but he wanted to do something a little more legit. Ashley had been proud that he sided with her on the business sense. However, because he still carried a weapon and didn't mind putting a nigga on his ass, he felt like he sided with Janahvi too. Either way, both of them had been proud, and that was all that mattered.

Jarell and Alanee walked side by side as they led his parents to a table in the VIP dining area. It was only reserved for the most elite, and that included Janahvi and Ashley Karter. When they got to the table, Jarell sat down with them and turned to Alanee, who still stood. "Baby, why don't you go in the kitchen and grab the best bottle of wine you can find?"

"Sure, Jarell. I'll be back."

As soon as she walked out, Jarell turned to his father and told him why he needed to see him.

"There's a nigga that works for you by the name of M'Baku Reynolds, runs with a killer that goes by the label Brightman. You know who I'm talking about?"

"Yeah. Bak works for me. He just don't know it. He a sarcastic mufucka. Feels like his shit don't stink. Why you asking about him?"

"I want you to cut off his supply."

Janahvi sat back in his chair and folded his chiseled arms over his chest. He looked to Ashley, as if he needed her permission to respond, because Jarell had never come at him like that before. Ashley nodded but kept quiet. Their son had always made sure to stay as far away as he could from his father's dealings, so they knew shit had to be serious.

"And what is your reasoning behind this request? You ain't never came at me this way before, so what's your beef about?"

Jarell hesitated because he knew his father was the best at detecting bullshit. He finally decided to just tell him the truth and hoped he would understand.

"Alanee."

Janahvi unfolded his arms and sat back up, closer to the table where he rested his elbows upon. "Nah, son, you gonna have to come a little better than that because I know you ain't trying to start a beef over another man's property."

"She's not his property. Nigga don't deserve something so genuine and valuable. He had his chance and fucked it up."

"Yeah, and you think you supposed to be the hero and save her? The fuck gonna happen when he comes back for her? Huh? You willing to risk your life over a woman you just met? Pussy got you gone already? You a mufuckin Karter, and I know your ass ain't that weak."

The words stung Jarell, but he knew his father was only looking out for his best interest. Janahvi was testing him to see just how deep he was feeling Alanee, but it was a test Jarell could pass with flying colors. He had never met a female before that made him feel the way Alanee did. From first glance, he knew that he would do anything to protect her.

"Yeah, Pops, I'm ready to risk everything for her. Do you remember when you told me that I'd know when I met the right one? Well, I met her, and ain't shit you or anyone else can do or say that could change how I'm feeling. Now, are you gonna cut that niggas shit off, or do I need to handle this another way?"

Janahvi nodded his head but didn't respond to Jarell's question. For his son to be ready to sit a nigga down about a woman told him that the shit had to be real. Jarell had done fucked around and fell in love, but that love would bring him enemies. Janahvi knew from experience that any love worth having was also worth fighting for. He thought back to the nigga he ultimately had to put to sleep. Kelvin Brown had been Ashley's ex-boyfriend, and no matter how hard she tried to get him out of her life, he just kept coming back. It was Janahvi's duty as a man to protect her and keep her safe, and he admired Jarell for wanting to step up for the woman he claimed to love.

"So, you really are feeling her like that? Enough to give your last breath if that's what it takes? But before I consider what you have requested of me, I have to ask you one more question. Would Alanee do the same for you?"

"You damn right I would."

All three of them turned their heads at the sound of her voice. Somehow, they had forgotten that she would be returning. She didn't know anything about the family business nor did she know just who Janahvi Karter was or how far his hand could reach. All she knew was that he was Jarell's father, and she was going to straighten his ass.

Jarell stood and was about to walk to her, but she held her hand up and shook her head to stop him. She went to the table and set the bottle of wine down and looked into the faces of the three of them.

"Alanee, how long have you been standing there?" Jarell asked because he wanted to know just how much she had heard.

"Long enough to know that you would die for me and long enough for your father to question my loyalty and love for you but it's something he doesn't need to worry about."

Ashley stood because she dared a bitch to talk to her son and husband that way. "You should really watch your tone of voice when you speak to a Karter man. It's obvious you don't know your place or mine."

"I apologize, Mrs. Karter, but you or your husband never have to second guess me when it comes to Jarell. I mean, I know we haven't been doing this for long, but it's been long enough for me to know that I don't ever want to be anywhere else. He has given me something that no one else ever could, and that's his heart. I would rather die than break it."

The room became eerily quiet as they absorbed her words. When Alanee turned to Jarell and looked him in the eyes, he pulled her into his arms. Janahvi put his hands in his pockets and let out a long sigh. Ashley could read him so well. She knew that he would honor Jarell's request. She thought about the consequences behind it and then suddenly remembered that Bak didn't even know who he worked for. She just hoped that would always remain true because if he ever found out that Jarell was the reason his supply had been cut off, shit could quickly get out of hand.

Janahvi was a smart man and had managed to stay off the radar, and she hoped it would continue to be that way. She'd be damned if the two people that mattered most in her life were to be jeopardized by one woman, especially one that had just entered their circle. She wondered what purpose cutting Bak off would serve since Alanee had already chosen Jarell. Ashley knew not to question her husband about his business in front of someone, including their son, so she didn't, but she had a few choice words for Alanee.

No one tried to stop her when she came from around the table and stood face to face with the woman who professed her loyalty to Jarell, a loyalty that Ashley felt was bullshit.

"There is no need for you to apologize because honestly, I don't want to hear it. You claim to have good intentions when it comes to my son, and I'm going to hold you to your word, but I will tell you this. If anything happens to him because of you, I will find you myself and kill you with my bare hands. Please do not doubt my words because I am a woman who stands by them. Now, if you'll excuse me."

Ashley turned and looked at Janahvi as if they had a secret code and then walked out of the room. He cleared his throat and nodded at Jarell. "I'll get with my people and see what I can do about your request."

He then walked out and left the couple standing there. Alanee had no clue of what had happened before she returned to the room. All she knew was that the bottle of wine she returned with was left untouched. She had been intimidated by Jarell's mother but admired the way she wanted to protect him. Something in her gut told her that his parents were very powerful people and to her that meant Jarell was more than he had been letting her believe. Either way, it didn't matter because she was where she wanted to be, and she could only hope that Bak didn't fuck that up.

Chapter Ten

"The fuck you mean there ain't nothin? I'm almost out, and you know I can't afford to run completely dry. Your ass better make mufuckin arrangements."

"Or what, Bak? I don't have the power to make shit happen for you right now, especially when I don't even know the reason for the cut off. I'm just the bitch in the middle. You're just gonna have to reach out and find another connect."

"Reach out? Bitch, if you wanna keep sitting on this dick, you'll find what I need."

"Nigga, please. Dick don't move me like the average bitch. I can get good dick anywhere. As a matter of fact, I got one in my bottom drawer."

From the first day that Bak had met Trameeka, he could tell that she was somebody important. He just couldn't put his finger on it. He knew that she had never gone anywhere and put in work, and yet she lived in the lap of luxury. He decided to ask her about it one day, but he thought her answer was bullshit.

"Ya know, Meeka, I ain't neva seen your ass go to work or anything, so how in the hell are you able to afford living like this? I mean, you always wearing that expensive ass, name brand shit and all. I ain't no dumb ass nigga, so what the hell you doing?"

"Actually, it really ain't your business, but since you feel like you need to know, I'll tell you. I live like this because my father made sure my future was secure before he was murdered. He made sure to leave plenty behind for me and my mother to live comfortably. I guess he wanted to make sure that neither one of us ever had to depend on a man."

"And you expect me to believe that you still living off that shit?"

"Look, Bak, my father was a boss, and everything he did was big. Besides, who the hell are you to question my funds when you ain't putting nothing in my Fendi bag?"

From that day on, he never questioned her finances again. He couldn't afford to fuck up what he had going with her because she ended up being his source for drugs. Bak sold dope like there was no tomorrow, but he had never invested his money. Instead, he tricked it off and bought things to impress the hoes. He tried to outshine niggas that had been in the game for years, but he would never be on their status. He needed the connect Trameeka had hooked up so to find out that his shit had been cut off had him in a foul mood.

"So, you really expect me to believe that you ain't got someone you can call and hook me up? Come on, there's got to be another connect."

"Look, Bak, we got lucky on the last one. I'm not the one that sells dope here. That's your profession. Why can't you get Brightman to pull some strings for you? As many dealers as he fools with, I'm sure that he can get someone to break you off."

"Break me off. Shit sounds like a fiend looking for a hit. A nigga like me needs quantity, not a break off."

"You know exactly what I meant, and he does enough for those hustlers, so I'm sure they would return the favor."

Bak, at first, felt like Trameeka was being funny, but the more he sat and thought about it, the more it made sense. It had been a minute since Brightman stepped out of the dope game, but he still put in work for the ones who were still in it. Because of him, so many rivals and enemies had been eliminated, so Bak was certain that Brightman had earned their favor. He couldn't believe that he hadn't thought of the idea himself.

"Ya know what? That's about the most sense you have ever made."

Bak pulled out his cell phone to call his right-hand man, and he answered on the first ring. It was almost as if he was expecting the call.

"Sup, nigga? The hell you at?"

"I'm over here with Meeka, but I need to see you about something. I'm kinda in a rut right now, and I'm hopin' you the nigga that can bail me out."

"Bet that up, my brotha. You know I got you. But there's some other shit I need to see you about. I found out some information you just might be interested in."

"Oh, yeah? What's it about, bruh? I could stand to hear something interesting right about now. Why don't you meet me at the condo? I'm about to jet there right now."

"I'm on my way."

Bak hung up and stood. His big frame towered over Trameeka as she laid in the bed. His gut told him that she could no longer be trusted, but he blamed it on his paranoia, something he had never been able to shake. She had never given him a reason to question her loyalty, so he just couldn't understand why he was on such high alert. She had never questioned him about his business or his whereabouts, and that was one of the things that had drawn him to her in the first place. She let him be a man, and he could do nothing but respect that, but something was definitely off. He intended to get to the bottom of it, but first, he had to meet up with his partner and find out just what the fuck was up.

"Now aren't you glad you listened to me? Brightman may actually turn out to be more of an asset than you ever thought."

"Yeah? Well, we about to find out."

Bak leaned over and kissed Trameeka on the forehead, something he always did before he walked out. He wasn't sure just what he was going to hear once he got to the condo, but he knew that Brightman heard a lot of shit when he was out on a job. A mufucka would tell you anything they could think of when that hard metal was pointed between their eyes.

Nine times out of ten, the information wouldn't even save them, but it was damn sure helpful to the one they gave it to.

Bak had always sworn that no matter how big the barrel was, he would never break. He would rather die a soldier than a pussy, but he also hoped that he would never be put in that position.

When he pulled up to the condo, Brightman was already there. Bak knew then that whatever he had to tell him had to be really serious. He turned off his ride and got out. The two friends gave each other dap and went into the condo. As soon as Bak closed the door behind them, he turned to Brightman and asked, "What's good, fam? What kind of shit got you beating me over here?"

Brightman sat down on the leather sofa and pulled out a fat blunt. His thirty-inch, diamond encrusted chain slid down his right side when he leaned back and struck the Bic. He inhaled hard and held the smoke as he pulled the black Ruger .380 from his waistline and set it on the couch beside him. He could tell that Bak was antsy and wanted to know what he had to tell him, but he would have to wait because Brightman was trying to get his high on first.

"Come on, nigga. The fuck you had me leave some good pussy for? I don't wanna sit here and watch your ass smoke some damn Kush. Tell me what the hell you got to say."

Brightman took one more pull from the blunt, and when he sat up, he let the smoke leave his lungs. He tried to pass it to Bak, but the only thing he wanted was the information that was supposed to be so damn interesting.

"Aiight, man, just chill because what I'm 'bout to tell you is gonna blow your fuckin mind more than this here Kush will."

"Well then spit that shit out. The fuck you waiting on?"

"Aiight, dawg. Did you know that you an impatient ass nigga?"

"Fuck, yo. Just get on with it."

"Well, word on the street is that the so-called waiter your little good girl, Lanee, is fucking with now is actually a very important mufucka. He ain't just part of the waitstaff either. He owns that place."

"Bruh, I think that shit you just smoked got your head all fucked up because I don't know why you telling me all this. What the fuck is you sayin?"

"Nigga, I'm trying to tell you that he is the key to the plug." Brightman paused and shook his head because he couldn't understand why Bak didn't get what he was saying, so he continued with what he had been told. "You ever heard of a nigga by the name of Janahvi Karter?"

Bak took a second to think about the question and then answered. "Ain't he the mufucka that used to have the whole city on lock?"

"Yeah, that's him, but ain't no used to shit. Come to find out, his ass is still running things."

"The fuck does that got to do with me? He ain't putting no bread on my table."

"Well, that's your own fault because that waiter sticking dick to your bitch is his son."

Bak got quiet for a minute, so he could absorb what Brightman had said. Jarell didn't seem like a thug, but he had learned long ago to never judge a book by its cover. "So, that nigga is in the game and bought a business to clean his money up."

"Nah, Bak. He ain't even part of his pops' business, but he does have a cousin who is."

"Look, Brightman, I ain't leave some warm pussy behind to come out here and try to figure out riddles. I need a new connect, and I very seriously doubt that waiter boy is going to hook me up with the big man, especially with Lanee in his ear."

"So, go through his cousin instead."

"And how in the hell do I get to his cousin?"

"Nigga, you just left the bitch."

Bak could not believe what he had heard, and then he remembered Jarell had brought up Trameeka's name. He had forgotten to ask her about him, but he would make it his business to do so.

He knew that the information Brightman had given him was true because a nigga like that always made sure his facts were straight. That meant Trameeka had been playing him the entire time he had been fucking with her. He wondered if Janahvi Karter had been the connect the whole time. If so, that would explain the sudden cut off and how Trameeka really found out about Alanee. He had hoped that she had kept shit between them real, but now, he wished he would have listened to his gut.

"So, Trameeka is that nigga's cousin? Ain't that some shit? I knew something had been off lately, but I never would have guessed it was something like this. The fuck I'm supposed to do now?"

"I say you play both of them bitches. You got five years invested with Alanee, so I know you know how to reel her in. She don't know that homeboy ain't just a waiter, and when she finds out he ain't kept that shit one thousand, she just might feel like some get back."

"Nah, she ain't gonna go for that. Lanee has always been a loyal bitch, and she don't have it in her heart to set somebody up and do 'em dirty. Not even a nigga like that. I fucked other bitches, and she still rode that shit with me. What he done ain't nothing compared to that. Besides, she's used to being spoiled, and even though I gave her all she desired, I can't even compete with a nigga of that status."

"Then you need to work on that source. Make the dick so good to her that she'll do anything you ask."

"I thought I already did that, but Trameeka ass is tough as a mufucka. It's like the bitch don't possess no feelings. Her heart is cold as ice. She don't even get jealous of those other bitches, and that's what drew me to her, but I am gonna ask her about the boss man and his seed."

"Bet that and just know that if shit don't turn out like you want it to, say the word because I keep my bitches loaded and ready."

Brightman picked his weapon up off the couch and put it back in the waist of his jeans and then stood. He knew that he had just put a lot on Bak, and he wanted to give him time to think about what position he would use. The two friends said their goodbyes, and when Brightman walked out, Bak decided to call Erica and sweet talk her because he needed her to help him put his plan in motion.

Chapter Eleven

"Ya know, Jarell? I got the feeling that your mother didn't like me very much, but she's not being fair because she don't even know me. She could at least give me a chance."

Jarell walked up to Alanee and wrapped his arms around her slim waist and kissed her on the cheek. He had to agree with her because his mother did act unfairly. He knew that it was only because she was worried about his best interest. It was crazy how quickly he had become attached to Alanee, but he trusted his gut with her and went with it. He couldn't allow a nigga from her past to interfere with what he was feeling, and even though she dissed him when they first met, he was glad that he continued to push forward because the payoff had been well worth it. He felt like he had finally found all that he had been looking for in her, and he could only hope that he never regretted it.

"Look, Lanee, I'm on your side, but I gotta be on my mom's side too. You gotta understand that you the first female I've introduced to my parents. That alone says a whole lot. All my mom is doing is looking out for me. She don't want me to rush into shit and get my heart broke, and for your sake, you may wanna abide by that. Wouldn't want Momma Dearest to beat that ass."

The two shared a laugh, and then, Jarell palmed her thong clad ass. Ever since the first night she gave herself to him, he couldn't get enough. He would live inside of her if he had the choice, but the time he could get would just have to do. Every time he was close to her, his dick rocked up, and it was no different that night, but the only issue was his cousin had called, so he didn't have time to wet it up. He kissed her pouty lips and backed up.

"Oh, you gonna tease a bitch and then run?"

"Hold that thought til I get back. I promise I ain't gonna keep you waiting long."

He kissed her once again and then walked out. Alanee really wanted his parents to be okay with their relationship. It had been one that she didn't even see coming. When she first met Jarell, she had felt a little chemistry, but she brushed it off because she was trying to be a loyal woman to Bak. She hoped that as long as she dissed Jarell, she could deny how she really felt. She blamed it on his occupational status, but deep inside, Alanee didn't give a damn about what he had. Material shit could be taken away fast and honestly didn't make her happy at the end of the day. Deep pockets could become shallow at any time, and to Alanee, real love didn't cost a thing. Bak had felt like he could do what he wanted to do, and all would be well once he went out and bought her something expensive or handed her a stack of bills when in reality, all she ever wanted was for him to admit his wrongdoing and apologize, but he had no remorse for doing her dirty.

Alanee was a rider and didn't mind having her man's back, but she needed a man who also had hers, and unfortunately, Bak did not turn out to be that man. He had only cared about himself and his own needs, but Jarell, he genuinely cared about her and actually put her feelings before his own. She felt like shit when she played hard to get and dissed him in the restaurant, and yet, when she needed someone the most, it was him who stepped up to the plate. She felt like she could trust him and depend on him for anything. He had been honest about everything and held no secrets, or so she thought.

She decided to sit back, relax, and watch her favorite show, *Wild 'N Out*, because a good laugh was just what she needed. No sooner than she propped her feet up, her cell phone rang. At first, she was going to ignore it but then decided to answer, just in case it was Jarell. She didn't even bother to look at the caller ID before she answered, but the person on the other end didn't even give her a chance to speak.

"Lanee, girl, I'm so glad you answered. Please don't hang up before you listen to what I got to say."

She couldn't believe that Erica had the nerve to call her. She didn't even know how she got her number because the phone was a new one. She was about to press end but decided against it. She did miss her friend and was curious as to what she had to say.

"What are you calling me for, Erica? There really isn't much you could say to me right now, but I will give you three minutes. After that, I'm hanging up and getting my number changed."

"Oh, Lanee, I'm so sorry. I know that I was dead wrong. There is so much I need to talk to you about, but I don't want to do it over the phone. Can we meet somewhere?"

"I don't have any transportation, Erica, and Jarell had to run to his cousin's, so I have no way to get anywhere."

"Oh, yeah, I forgot. Well, tell me where you are and I'll come to you."

Alanee wasn't sure if she should let Erica know where she was at because she didn't know how Jarell would feel about it, but her heart pounded in anticipation of seeing her best friend again. Erica had always been there for her through all of her ups and downs, and she hated that they had fallen out over a no-good ass nigga like Bak. Men were easy to come across, but friends were rare, and she didn't want to lose the only one she had.

"Okay, but you better not ever tell Bak where I'm staying. Jarell would kill me."

"Girl, I don't fuck with his big ass no more either. That bastard dissed me in front of a room full of people and to think I lost you over that bullshit I pulled with him."

Alanee gave her the address and then went to the bedroom and slid on a pair of pajama shorts over her thongs. She came to Jarell with nothing but the clothes on her back, but he made sure to fill up a closet just for her. When she asked him how he could afford to do all that, he told her that he had a nice little savings account stashed, and there was no reason why she shouldn't believe him. No sooner than she walked out of the bedroom, she heard the buzzer that alerted her to someone at the front door. She had to admit that she was nervous because of all that had happened between her and Erica, but she felt like she'd be okay once the awkwardness was over with.

She slid the locks on the door back and opened it to Erica's smiling face, and all her anger went away. "Oh, Erica, I've missed you so much."

They shared a hug, and then, Erica stepped inside the penthouse. She was in awe of its beauty and just stood there for a minute, so she could take it all in. She thought about what Bak had told her concerning Jarell, but she still didn't expect what she had walked into.

"Damn, Lanee, your ass done moved up for real. Bitch, this is the fuckin penthouse suite, and only a baller could afford something like this. Girl, I knew that restaurant was just a cover up. That nigga is caked the fuck up."

"Erica, please. Jarell's just been saving his money. That's why he is able to live like this."

"Well, I don't know about all that, but he definitely has a bigger bag than your last nigga, bitch. Bak would really be fucked up if he knew you were living this large."

"Whatever. I wouldn't give a damn how Bak feels about shit. I can't believe I stuck with him for so long. What the hell was I thinking?"

"No, what was I thinking? I'm sorry I went behind your back like that. I was dead ass wrong, but if we can still be friends, I'll never do no shit like that again."

"I never stopped being your friend, Erica. I was just so hurt when I went over there and saw you. Why did you do it?"

"Honestly, Lanee, you're perfect and always have been, and I guess that I could say I looked up to you and always wanted to be in your shoes, but niggas just didn't take to me like they did you. It was always like I was the ugly stepsister, and no one noticed me. I thought that by stepping in your place with Bak, it would make me feel more important and cared about, but that shit only made me feel worse. I can't lie though. The dick was good."

"Yeah, I know, and I think that's what made me stick around for so long. Ya know Bak was my first, so I didn't have anyone to compare him to, but now, I have Jarell. I feel like I can just sit here and chill without having to worry about him running to another bitch, and it's all because of you, Erica. I'm glad you encouraged me to call him because he is truly Heaven sent."

"I'm so happy for you, and I hate to burst your bubble, but girl, don't get too grand because he ain't all you think he is. As a matter of fact, he ain't who you thought he was at all."

"What the hell are you talking about?"

"Oh, Lanee. You have always been so blinded by your search for love until you can't see anything else."

"And just what the hell do I not see? Please don't start with that bullshit, Erica. We just made up."

"Like I've told you so many times before, I verify my facts before I bring them. I don't tell you things to hurt you, Lanee. I tell you to try and keep you from getting hurt, and no matter what we been through, I'ma still look out for you."

"Whatever it is, just go ahead and tell me. Can't nothing be worse than what I just went through with Bak."

"Okay, but you gonna want to sit down because what I got to say is going to knock you off your feet."

Alanee shook her head and sat down on the plush sofa. Her and Erica had only made up minutes earlier and here she came with the hood gossip but what worried her the most was the fact that Erica's gossip usually turned out to not be gossip at all. Jarell seemed to be a breath of fresh air, and that was just what she needed in her life. The last thing she wanted was to hear something that could possibly change all that. Erica sat down beside her and told her everything that Bak had told her to say.

"Lanee, you do know that Jarell really ain't no waiter at that restaurant. He only pretended to be, so he could try to hook up with you."

"Really, Erica? I do work there now, remember? He does work there, so you gonna have to come better."

"Okay then. Jarell is your boss, bitch. He owns that motherfucker. You didn't find it kinda funny that you didn't even have to interview for that position?"

"He said he was cool with the boss, and I was hired off of his word."

"Uh, he is cool with the boss because he runs that place, and since I told you that much, ain't no sense in me stopping now. Girl, that nigga is a millionaire, and his father, Nahvi Karter, with his fine ass, ranks up there with the biggest of kingpins. He's like the Black version of El Chapo, and all this was funded by a cocaine empire."

Alanee could feel the tears as they formed in her eyes, but there was no way she would let them fall in front of Erica. She couldn't believe what she had heard. Jarell promised that he would always be straight up with her and never keep any secrets, but he turned out to be just like Bak. Her mind started to play tricks on her and made her wonder if he really went to see his cousin or did he run to another bitch. There was no way her heart could handle any more hurt.

"Look, Erica, I appreciate you looking out for me, but right now, I think I just need to be alone. What you just told me is a lot to process. So, can we just hook up another time?"

"I understand, and I'm sorry again for all that has happened. Don't be too hard on Jarell though because maybe he had his reasons for not being completely honest with you.

He seems like such a good guy, and I think he should be given the benefit of the doubt. Call me tomorrow so we can go hang out."

Alanee shut the door and then leaned up against it. She felt so let down and wasn't sure how she was going to handle the situation. She didn't understand why Jarell didn't tell her everything about himself. He had promised her that if she gave him a chance, he would be completely open to her, but he had broken that promise. She didn't know how she could have been so blind. He lived in the lap of luxury, and she believed him when he told her it was from money he had saved up. Alanee knew that when shit seemed too good to be true, it usually was, and still, she fell for it.

She would be a nervous wreck until he made it home, and then, she could find out all the answers to her questions, but there was nothing she could do about it until then. She decided to go run a tub full of warm water and soak in some bubbles to help clear her mind, but no sooner than she plugged the drain, the doorbell buzzed again.

"Dammit, Erica. I told you I wanted to be alone."

Alanee rushed to the door and opened it, so she could give Erica a piece of her mind. Her friend had always been hardheaded and didn't want to listen, but Alanee needed some time to herself to absorb all the information she had told her, but it wasn't Erica on the other side.

"Jarell, I thought you went to see your cousin. What are you doing here?"

Jarell gave her a funny look because he could tell that she had been expecting someone else, and that thought didn't sit right with him. He had told her when he picked her up that night that she could stay as long as she wanted, but the only rule he had was not to tell anyone where she resided. He had managed to keep where he laid his head on the low, and he was going to be pissed if she had gone against what he asked.

"I live here, remember? But since you acting like you was expecting someone else, that must mean someone else has been up in my shit."

He walked up close to her, which caused her heart to pound in fear, but she never needed to be afraid when it came to him because he would rather die than bring harm to her, and he also wouldn't allow anyone else to.

"I'm sorry, Jarell. I know you told me not to let anyone know where you stayed, but Erica somehow found out my new number and called me. She's my only friend, and I ain't gonna lie. I missed her and wanted to see her, so I told her to come over. She only left about ten minutes ago. I thought that maybe she forgot something and came back. Please don't be mad at me. I needed to see her."

He took a second to think about what she had said. His nose flared in anger because his safe haven had now been compromised, and he didn't like that. There could be a lot of consequences that he would have to face behind it. One of the things he loved about her was her forgiving heart, but she tended to forgive the wrong people. He turned around and shut the front door and then turned back to her. He could tell from the look in her eyes that she had questions. About what, he wasn't sure, but he would tell her anything she wanted to know. He brushed his hand over her cheek and bent down to kiss her, but she pulled back from him. He hadn't been ready for the gesture, but he needed to know the reason behind it.

"The fuck is up with that?"

"Jarell, you and I need to talk about what Erica came over here for."

"Aiight. Well, go ahead and spit that shit out. I'm ready for it."

"When was you gonna tell me that you were my boss?"

He laughed at the question because honestly, to him, it was a childish one. "Your boss, huh? Just so you know, I never looked at you like an employee because I always felt like you was my equal. The first day I saw you, you was outside with that nigga, and you wasn't having a lovely conversation. When you came with your friend, you didn't ask me shit. You automatically assumed I was a lowly worker, and you ain't even want to give me the time of day, but when you finally gave in, I wanted it to be because you really felt me, even though you still thought I was that lowly waiter you dissed."

"That is such a tired ass reason, and it is not a good excuse for why you didn't tell me you owned the place."

"Does it matter? Would it have made a difference if you would have known upfront that I got long money? Would you have treated me like somebody then since that shit meant so much to you? Huh? Does it excite you that I'm a rich mufucka?"

"You having money or not had never been an issue. That's not the kind of person I am, and you know that. I'm hurt because you have hid who you really are from me, and I feel like I don't even know you now. Makes me wonder what else you got to hide."

"I don't got shit to hide, and I never did. You just never seemed real concerned with anything but having a man that meets your standards. Remember? I was a downgrade."

"That's not fair, Jarell, and you know it."

"Look, Lanee, I'm a grown ass man, and I need a grown ass woman in my life. This shit right here is childish, and I ain't playing these fucking games with you. I ain't that nigga you left behind. If you wanna push on because I own a fucking business, then you do that but make sure that's what you really want because my door don't revolve."

His words stung her like a bee, but she felt like he was bluffing. She wasn't sure if she should take her chances or not, but she didn't want to look like a weak fool. She was tired of men having control of her heart, so the choice she made had to be the right one. She figured that since she had already dug the hole, she might as well keep the shovel going.

"I know about your father too. I know everything."

The look Jarell gave her caused chills to climb her spine, and suddenly, the fear in her deepened. She hadn't known him that long, so she didn't know what he was capable of. As soon as the words left her mouth, she regretted them, but it was too late to take them back.

"Get your shit and get the hell outta my space."

"I'm sorry, Jarell."

"Nah, your ass ain't sorry, but if anything comes my father's way, you will be. You obviously ain't what I thought you were."

"Guess that makes us even."

Alanee picked up her purse and cell phone and walked out, not knowing what her next move would be. She stood with her phone in hand for a minute and finally decided where she would go. She dialed the number quickly and was relieved when the caller picked up on the first ring.

Chapter Twelve

All Jarell thought about on the drive to Trameeka's was the argument he'd had with Alanee. He didn't care that she knew everything about him and his family, but he had wanted to be the one who told her, not someone else, especially someone who meant her no good. His feelings for her had grown stronger, and deep down, he didn't mean anything he said. He finally found his other half and had fucked it up already, but he didn't need a woman who couldn't stand by his side when shit got dropped. He needed one that put a mufucka in their place when they stepped out of it.

He pulled into Trameeka's driveway, and before he got out, she was at his car door with a smile. She had always been more like a big sister to him than a cousin, and he would risk his own life to protect her, but he was pissed and needed some questions answered. He got out and slammed the door and hugged her like always, but the hug was missing something, and she could tell the difference.

"Hey, what's going on with you? That wasn't a normal greeting."

"Aye, we got some shit to talk about, and you ain't gonna like it."

"Okay, let's go inside."

Jarell followed her into the expensively decorated house. Trameeka had done really well for herself, and he was proud of her. The money that her father had left behind was spent very well, but he didn't have time to admire his surroundings. He had to find out where the information about his family was leaked. No sooner than she shut the front door, he went in.

"The fuck have you been telling that nigga?"

"What the hell are you talking about, Jarell?"

"Lanee knows about my father and his business dealings. Said that bitch, Erica, told her and the only person she could have got that information from is that nigga, Bak, so you got some mufuckin explaining to do."

"Fuck you, Jarell. I ain't gotta explain shit to you or nobody else because I ain't told a damn thing. Do you really believe that I would do that? Because if you do, then you can turn around and get the hell out of my house. You know me better than that so don't come up in my shit and question me about a damn thing."

"Yeah, well, how does he know then? Huh? Erica has been fuckin that nigga too, so you sure that shit ain't come out in some pillow talk?"

"Pillow talk? Please. Bak is just a piece of dick that I enjoy and nothing else. The only pillow talk I give him is when he ain't fucking me hard enough."

"You know your ass is real funny, but you sleeping with the enemy, and you know it's wrong. What type of message does that send?"

"He wasn't the enemy until you started fucking his bitch. What's the matter, Jarell? What are you afraid of?"

"I ain't afraid of shit, but my pops has managed to keep his business quiet for all these years and for you to allow a dirty dick ass nigga to come up in here and convince you to tell him everything is a stab in the back. How will you feel if something happens to my father? What's wrong, Meeka? You mad cause it's your old man that ate that bullet instead of mine?"

"You bastard. I love Uncle Nahvi as if he were my own father, and I would rather die a slow, torturous death than to be disloyal to him. In case you haven't forgotten, it's me that backs him up in his street affairs because he has a pussy for a son. Why don't you just go run your little restaurant and let me worry about what happens from here?"

Jarell shook his head and then walked out. Him and Trameeka had never fell out about anything before, and he knew that he was just feeding off of his emotions. She had shown mad loyalty to Janahvi all of her life, and even though

Jarell knew better than to think that she would betray him, he had to blame somebody. He decided to go by his parents' house, so he could warn his father about his business being out.

He pulled up to the gated, lavish estate and parked. He had always wondered why they needed such a big house, but he never got the nerve up to ask them. They lived in the house by themselves but still felt the need to furnish all seven bedrooms. On occasion, him or Trameeka would go spend the weekend with them, and even his Auntie Tracey when she would be in town, but other than that, the rooms were never used. He admired their sense of style, but it was still too much for him.

Jarell had never been a flashy nigga. He saw no sense in it. He had always thought that it brought too much attention, and since he was a loner, that was the last thing he wanted. He was fine with his two-bedroom penthouse, where he felt like he was hidden from the world, but now, his secret was out. Alanee had been the only female he had ever taken there. All the other bitches he had fucked got finessed in a hotel room or an apartment that he had leased out just for that purpose. He just never felt like anyone had been special enough for him to take home, much less move into his space, but Alanee had somehow penetrated the depths of his heart. He really hadn't meant anything he said when he lashed out on her and hoped that when he got home, she would be there, waiting for him. He couldn't even imagine going back to a life that didn't include her, but he had made his own bed. Jarell had been so lost in his thoughts that he forgot where he was until he heard the knock at his window.

"Jarell, honey, are you okay in there?"

He looked up and saw the woman who had given him life and love. She was the epitome of what all women should be, and his father was the man lucky enough to have her. Janahvi and Ashley's love had been one for romance books because it was real and solid. Jarell couldn't imagine anything coming along and destroying what they had built.

He often wondered if his father would get tired of getting his hands dirty. The dope game was Janahvi's passion, but Jarell was worried that one day, it would either kill him or rob him of his freedom. He couldn't imagine living that kind of life himself. That was why he always turned his father down when he invited him to the table for a plate of what he was serving. Jarell decided that he would rather be hungry than live a life constantly looking over his shoulder and wondering when he would be taken down by his enemies.

Jarell smiled at his mother and got out. She quickly pulled him in for a hug, as if she hadn't seen him in forever. For a small woman, she had a tight grip, but he always welcomed it.

"I'm cool, Ma. You don't need to worry about me. I just got a lot of shit going through my mind right now."

"It's that damn girl, ain't it?"

"Come on, Ma. Cut her some slack. Believe it or not, Lanee reminds me of you in a lot of ways. Just give her a chance and get to know her, aiight?"

"Mmm hmm. I'll think about it, but I'm not making any promises. Come on. Your father is inside, and if I'm reading him right, he's been waiting on you to show up."

The two of them walked up the concrete pathway that led to the front door, but Janahvi had already opened it and walked out to greet his only heir. Jarell could tell from the look on his face that he already knew why he was there and charged the warning of his arrival on Trameeka. Ashley knew that her presence wouldn't be needed, so she kissed her son on the cheek and left him with his father. Janahvi did his best to keep her out of his affairs because he didn't want to give anyone a reason to use her as bait, but Ashley was fine with being left out of the loop. She only hoped that one day, Janahvi would grow tired and get out of it too.

When Ashley was out of earshot, Janahvi nodded his head to the chairs that were perched on the porch. Jarell sat down and looked up into his father's eyes. The last thing he ever wanted was to disappoint him, and since he was hard to read, Jarell wasn't sure what he was thinking, but he would soon find out.

Janahvi looked at his seed and saw himself deep inside of him. Him and Ashley had done well, but he felt like Jarell still had some things to learn, but he couldn't teach unless the student was willing to listen.

"I just talked to your cousin, and I didn't like what I heard, but I'ma let you spit your side of it out before I make a judgement call."

"Ah, Pops, Meeka knows I ain't mean that shit I gave to her. I was talking out of my emotions because I ain't gonna lie; the thought of something coming at you or Mom because of me makes me wanna kill a mufucka."

"And you shall but only when the time calls for it. A nigga can only get as close to me as I let them so don't think they got one up on us. Sometimes, you gotta shake some shit up to show 'em who runs the show. It's obvious that the little nigga don't know how to keep his mouth shut, but my question to you is can ya girl zip hers?"

"What the fuck kind of question is that, and why are you asking me it?"

"The camp has been compromised, and it wasn't by your cousin. I sent that word out because I hear that big mufucka been talking some shit since you been with his woman."

"She ain't his woman anymore."

"But she was when you stepped to her and don't look at me like that because I have eyes and ears everywhere. When you sneeze, I know about it. Do you think when he kicked her out, he expected her to run to another man? Hell no. He expected her to come back and beg for another chance, but you stepped in the way, and now, that makes you the enemy. Now that he knows you're my son, I'm the enemy too, but he don't seem to comprehend what he's up against." Janahvi took a breath of air and thought about his next question before he asked it and hoped Jarell answered it with the truth. "Are you in love with this girl?"

Jarell didn't even have to think about his response because he knew that he loved Alanee. "Yeah, Pops. I do love her, and I know I should have been straight up with her at first, but I just needed to make sure she was there because of me, not because of what I represented. It wasn't no one else's place to tell her anything."

"But they did, and you can't fault her for being hurt and angry but pushing her out of your life wasn't the right move. Now you gonna sit and sulk, wondering if she went back to what was familiar, but I'm here to tell you that if she does, then she was never meant to be yours in the first place."

Jarell knew that he was right, but it didn't help ease how he felt. He didn't know how he would react if he found out that Alanee ran back to Bak. He didn't want a woman that he felt he had to run after and question her feelings. She had to be able to stand up and take the bad along with the good. Their days wouldn't always be great, and when he fell weak, he would need her strength to pick himself back up. Was Alanee that woman was a question that only her actions could answer.

"So, you saying if she runs back to that nigga, I'm just supposed to let him have her."

"She's not a piece of property, son. She is a human being with real feelings, and you are supposed to protect them, not step on 'em. If she's there when you get home, then you embrace it. Let her know how you really feel and don't ever keep anything else from her again. But if she ain't back, then you just gonna have to let her go and move on."

"And what about that nigga?"

"Oh, we gonna handle him, no matter what the lady chooses, but we gonna have to get his sidekick first. Brightman comes from a line of ruthless killers, and I don't know about you, but I'm trying to keep breathing. Now, go on home and get your answers but have your gun ready because when it's time to move, I'ma need you to come out blastin."

Chapter Thirteen

"So, when we gonna make that move on the nigga? I'm ready to take what should have been given."

"Chill, Bak. You know I gotta make sure that everything is in place first. If we move too fast, we could fuck the whole thing up and lose everything. Besides, you ain't even heard back from that bitch, Erica, yet."

"I don't know what's up with that, but the dumb bitch ain't called or nothing. I can't even believe she fell for it. She actually thinks I'ma wife her ass."

"Yeah, she fell for that shit real quick. I told you. All you had to do was pipe her down just right, and she would believe anything. But what you gonna do when it's all said and done, and you run off into the sunset with Alanee and all Karter's money? You think she just gon' sit back and be cool with it?"

"Fuck that bitch. She gonna fuck around and swallow a bullet fucking with me. She don't run a damn thang here but that dick sucker, which is what she should be on her knees doing right now."

Bak and Brightman shared a laugh, but Erica didn't find shit funny. She had walked in on their conversation without them even knowing it. She decided to not make her presence known until she felt like they were done plotting. She would take in every word they said and use it as ammunition. She couldn't believe that she had fucked up her friendship with Alanee for Bak's no good ass when all along, he had been playing her. After she thought about what she had told Alanee, she caught on to what Bak's purpose was. He thought that he could actually get Alanee back by dropping dimes on Jarell, but Erica planned to be one step ahead of him.

The room had grown quiet for a minute, but Bak broke the silence after he lit a blunt. "So, how we gonna pull it off? You know it's gonna be hard as hell getting to the big man."

"That's why you gon' get that bitch, Trameeka, to pull you right on in."

"I don't know, bruh. That bitch smart as hell. I mean, I been fucking that bitch for almost a year and never put what she had going on together. She had me believing my shit was coming from a foreign mufucka when, the whole time, it was her damn uncle. Shit been on her doorstep, and I just kept stepping over it."

"Well, now that you know, make her ass hook you up, and if she don't wanna comply, we follow her ass to the nigga's compound and take it from there. But like I said before, we can't move too fast. Janahvi Karter been around a long time, and he moves in silence, so each step we make has to be carefully calculated."

Erica had heard enough, so she turned around and quietly opened the front door back up and then slammed it closed. She wanted to make it appear like she had just walked in. She knew Bak would want to know how things went with Alanee, but since he wanted to play games with her, she would play along. She had always been a good liar. In fact, she was the best, and she would use an Oscar worthy performance on Bak. She walked over to him and pulled the blunt from between his lips and took a drag. She inhaled the smoke and then straddled him, and when she let the smoke go, she put her lips to his and blew it in his mouth. When he released it, he went in a rage that wouldn't last long because a nigga would listen to anything when some pussy was involved in the equation.

"Bout damn time you showed your ass back up. The fuck took you so long?"

"Nigga, you know it wasn't easy getting back in Lanee's good graces. I fucked her nigga, and it's hard to come back from that, and then to turn around and try to convince her that her new man was keeping secrets was a lot of work."

"She ask about your business with me?"

"Of course, she did, but I told her I was done with your sorry ass, and she fell for it."

"So, if she fell for it then that means she gon' leave that nigga."

"Why do you care if she leaves him or not? You got me now, and you know I'ma ride."

"Hmm, I know you straddling this beast like you ready to put in some work."

"Now you know I stay ready, so why don't you get rid of ya boy, so I can clock in? I think a bitch like me deserves a little raise too."

Bak looked over at Brightman and winked, but he didn't have to because his boy already knew what was up.

"Don't worry bout me, Bak. I got shit to do anyway, so I'ma head on out and finish working on our little project. Holla at me later."

"Aiight, later, mane."

As soon as Erica heard the front door slam, she began to ask more than Bak was willing to answer. "So, what kind of project are you and Brightman doing? You know I don't mind getting my hands a little dirty."

"Nah, this ain't no job for a female, so you need to direct that energy to this dick."

She unzipped his pants and pulled his manhood out. She slid her hand up and down his shaft slowly and then kissed him, hoping it would make him talk more.

"Ah, come on, Bak. You know I ain't gonna say shit. You have to be plotting on something since you made me go tell Lanee that stuff about her man."

"That nigga ain't her man and don't let me hear you say that shit again."

She jumped off of his lap and stood over him with her hands on her hips. "Why you being so defensive about me calling Jarell her man when that's what he is?"

Bak sat there as his nose flared in anger. Every time he thought about the nigga sliding up in Alanee, he wanted to murder somebody. She had been his for so long, and he never thought she would really move on. Erica couldn't even hold a candle to what Alanee was to him, but she was on hand pussy, and that was what he needed at that time.

"Oh, yeah, well, don't forget that I was still her man when that nigga came along but that didn't stop his ass, so when I reach back in for mine, he better sit his ass down."

"What you mean when you reach back in? I thought you wanted to be with me, Bak. That's what you said, or was it a lie, so I would go along with your bullshit to make Lanee leave Jarell?"

"You actually thought that a nigga like me would wife a gutta slut like you? Bitch, you an embarrassment to my swag and my set up so get the hell outta here with that bullshit you talking."

"Or what? I heard what you and Brightman were talking about when I walked in, and if you smart, you'll act right when it comes to me because I'll be that bitch that blows your whole spot up."

Bak ran up on her and put his hand around her throat, a move that Erica didn't expect. "Bitch, don't you ever threaten me. All I wanna do is eat, but because of that nigga, I'm hungry now, and I'll be damned if he gets away with it. He stole my bitch and my bank. and he has to pay for that, so if you know what I know, you'll keep that mouth shut."

"I'm not scared of you, Bak, and neither is Jarell. Alanee finally found a man that's worthy of her, and if you're smart, you'll leave her alone and let her be happy. I can assure you that you don't wanna go against him because just like you did with Lanee, you will lose."

"Oh, yeah? Well, you wasn't too worried about her being happy when you was ridin' this dick, so you shouldn't worry about it now."

Bak finally let her go, and she slid down the wall while holding her throat. Erica wasn't scared of death because she couldn't think of anything she had to live for. The only family she had was her mother, but she was so busy living her own life that sometimes she acted like Erica didn't even exist. Her mother probably wouldn't even notice if she never went home.

"She's not going to take you back. I give you my word on that. Even if you kill Jarell and get away with it, she would never go back to your sorry ass. And when she finds out everything you're up to, she is going to hate you. I can't wait to tell her."

Bak pulled a gun from his waistband and pointed it at her, but she could tell that he was nervous by the way his hand shook. "How you gonna tell something with a bullet in your chest?"

"Go head, Bak, pull the trigger, you coward. You can't do it. Can you? You're a fuckin pussy, and you gonna get your shit split when you run up on Jarell. Mark my words, fuck boy."

Bak pulled the trigger, but nothing happened. He wasn't as experienced with guns as Brightman, and he didn't have time to check it, so he turned the weapon over and hit Erica in the dome. The gash it left behind knocked her out, and the blood began to pool under her, which caused Bak to panic. The thought of evidence being left in his house made him regret his decision. He decided to cover her body up until he went and handled some business, and then, he would clean up. He grabbed a blanket out of his bedroom and threw it over her and then walked out.

He got in his ride and sat there for a minute. He hated that he had to do Erica that way, but he wasn't about to let her fuck up what he had planned. He had struggled enough in the dope game, and just when he thought he was on top, he had another obstacle to face. He refused to sit back and starve while the next man's plate was full. He started the car, and before he drove away, he put in his favorite song, *The Struggle*. He bopped his head to the beat while the voice of Pimpin352 filled the air. "Before my folks starve, I bet your family won't eat. Many nights I didn't sleep, they got a pot, I want a piece. So, I had to run that bread up. It ain't no handouts to be given. If you a street nigga, you know how I'm living. So, I had to run that bread up, and I take the Lord as my witness. Before I starve, any nigga can get it."

Bak felt like it was time to take what should have been his. He had been a street nigga all his life, and yet, he was still at the bottom of the totem pole. He was tired of being treated like a nobody, and it was time them niggas put some respect on it. He wasn't some ditch diggin ass punk who mufuckas thought they could treat any kind of way.

He drove as fast as he could to his destination and was thankful that the crackers were nowhere in sight. He couldn't afford to get cased up, especially for speeding. His drug supply had run out, so he wasn't worried about that. He needed to know what to expect when it came to Janahvi and Jarell Karter, and he knew just where to go to get that information.

When he pulled into Trameeka's driveway, he noticed that she had already come outside. It was almost as if she was expecting him to show up. He cut off the engine and slowly exited his ride because he wasn't sure what to expect. He had come too far to be pushed back by some pussy problems, but a nigga needed to know that when they hit, he would hit back.

He walked carefully and cautiously to the front porch steps and made sure to keep a grip on the handle of his gun, the same one that he had just used to knock Erica out.

"Why you got your hand on your piece, Bak? Ain't shit going down here, so you can relax."

He let the handle go and noticed a little blood on his fingers. He wondered how Trameeka would feel if she saw it. He didn't feel like explaining anything to her because he wasn't sure if she would freak out or not. True enough, she seemed like a soldier, but to him, a bitch was still a bitch.

"Aye, you by yourself up in there?"

"Come on, Bak, really? Why you acting all paranoid and shit?"

"Shouldn't I be? It seems you been keeping some shit on the down low, so now, I don't know what to expect. You wanna put me up on the shit going on with that nigga you ain't tell me was your people?"

"There's nothing to put you up on, and that nigga you referring to can kiss my ass."

"Oh, yeah? You expect me to believe that's how you really feel? You think I'm dumb."

"No, Bak. I don't think that, but it's obvious that my cousin thinks I am. He had the nerve to come over here and check me about you finding out that my uncle is the plug. I don't like to be accused of shit I'm not guilty of."

"Yeah, about that. How long was you gonna let me believe that I was cut off?"

"You were cut off, Bak. None of that was a lie, but you have nothing to worry about because I'ma get you put back on. My cousin thinks he runs shit, but I'ma show him I'm not included in that."

"So, what you got planned?"

"Why don't you come on inside and give a girl what she's been craving, and then, maybe we can share some pillow talk."

Bak smiled and walked up the porch steps while Trameeka pulled the tie on her silky robe. It fell to the ground in a small pile at her feet, but she didn't care. All she cared about was having him inside of her. She loved the time that she spent with Bak, and she wanted to enjoy every second she could because she knew that one day, it would all come to an end.

Chapter Fourteen

Jarell wasn't sure what to expect when he made it home, but he hoped that when he opened the door, Alanee would be there, waiting for him. The elevator ride up felt like it took longer than ever before, but he charged it to him being anxious. His father had been right about everything he said, which usually ended up being the case. Jarell knew that there was a chance Alanee would run back to Bak, and if she had, then he could only blame himself. Bak never deserved a woman like her, and it pissed Jarell off to think about the bastard ever touching her again. The closer he got to his door, the harder his heart pounded. He pulled out his key and gripped it tightly, but before he had a chance to push it into the keyhole, the door opened, and Alanee greeted him with a smile. He reached out and pulled her into his arms and held her tightly. It was as if they had gone years without seeing each other when in all actuality, it had only been hours.

"My God, I didn't think you'd be here when I came back."

"Well, honestly, Jarell, I did think about staying gone, but the feelings I have inside for you wouldn't let me. I can't lie. I'm in love with you, and you may feel like it's too soon for me to say that, but I couldn't imagine living a life without you in it. I'm sorry that I listened to Erica and overreacted. After I thought about it, I came to the conclusion that I acted the way she hoped I would."

"Nah, Ma, you ain't did nothing wrong. I should have been told you everything, and I had planned to, but I kept putting it off because I really didn't think it was a big deal."

"How could you not know it was a big deal? Jarell, you should know by now that I don't care about your money and your material things. I don't care that you come from street royalty. Yeah, I know I talked a lot of shit about you when we first met, but it was only because I was feeling you. I had a man, and I knew I couldn't act on it, so the easy thing for me to do was push you away."

"Well, I guess you see that I'm a hard mufucka to get rid of."

"And I am happy about that because I would have lost out to the next bitch because of my own selfish choices. I can't even imagine you being with someone else, especially if it would have been my fault. There was no way I could let you slip away."

"You'll never have to worry about anything like that because you are it for me. Shit, I need someone I can lay down with and not have to worry about putting a rubber on it. You that someone cause you the only bitch that makes me wanna cum inside. The first time I laid eyes on you, I knew I wanted you in my life, and I wasn't walking away without you."

"How did you even know I would give in?"

Jarell held his arms out to his sides and did a complete turn. "Ain't no way you could have resisted all of this. I knew you were going to be mine, and I like to believe that I'm the reason you have that big smile on your face."

"Yeah, Jarell, you are the reason, but there is one other thing that can make me smile like this." Alanee reached down and unzipped his jeans, so she could get to what brought her extreme pleasure. She had never thought it could get any better than Bak, but once she allowed Jarell inside of her, she knew she had finally found Heaven. What she thought was love hadn't been love at all until he came into her life. She understood his reasoning behind not telling her everything, and she couldn't blame him. He had only wanted to make sure she was with him for all the right reasons.

Alanee giggled and turned her back to him and walked away. He didn't know what was so funny, but he was about to give her something to wipe the smirk off of her face. He followed behind her and noticed on his walk that every few steps, there was a piece of clothing on the floor. He shrugged his shoulders and began to take his clothes off too. Piece by piece, he threw them on the floor until he made it to the bedroom.

"Okay, so this is what we doing, but I can live with it."

He opened the bedroom door and saw that Alanee was already on the bed. Her thick, mocha-colored thighs were spread while her garden was open and ready for him to plant some seeds. She had his dick so hard he swore it would burst. He had never met a female that turned him on as much as she did. Alanee was a rare breed, and he felt like the luckiest man alive. Bak had been a fool to let her slip away, but he didn't plan on making the same mistake. He had almost fucked up once already and was glad that it didn't cost him in the end.

"You standing there, staring. Dick all hard and ready to put in some work. I'm trying to figure out how all this pussy is in your face, and yet you haven't made a move to touch it."

Alanee licked her bird finger and then pushed it in between her pussy lips. She rotated her hips while she massaged her swollen bud. Ever since she took Erica's advice and touched herself, she couldn't get enough. She couldn't believe that she had never explored her own sexuality in that way, and she enjoyed it even more when she did it for Jarell. Being with him helped her find her inner prowess. He made her feel freaky and comfortable enough to do things she had never done before.

"A real nigga like me likes taking his time, so he can enjoy such delicacies as yourself."

He walked closer to the bed, so he could get a better view. Her performance was amazing, but he could only handle a few minutes of it. He crawled on the bed between her legs and did something he had never done before.

"Oh, Jarell, baby, you gonna make me cum."

He pulled her swollen clit between his lips and teased it with his tongue. He hoped that he was doing it right because he never had a training manual to teach him. He had always wanted to do it, just to see what it was like, but there was never anyone he cared enough about to put his mouth on. So many young women had already been mutted out and didn't care who ran up in them. So, he knew he would have to be careful, but Alanee was a true lady. She had only been with M'Baku Reynolds, and Jarell figured that nigga wasn't man enough to take care of a woman's needs before his own. Bak was too selfish, but Jarell didn't mind taking over and doing his dirty work. He could tell that he was doing something right because of the way Alanee was talking.

"Damn, Jarell, that feels so good. Shit, you about to make me cum. Baby, I want you inside of me, so I can cum all over that dick. Come on, baby, please."

Jarell wanted to keep tasting her sweet essence on his tongue, but he had to agree with her. He wanted to get inside of her wetness, and he could wait no longer. He let her swollen pearl go and looked in her eyes as he hovered over her. Her nakedness was a beautiful sight, and he knew that he would never get tired of looking at it. Alanee was perfection, and he wanted to embrace each and every part of her. He felt like it was as close to paradise as he would ever get. He was about to slide inside of her but changed his mind and laid down beside her instead.

"What the hell are you doing, Jarell? You can't just make me feel like that and then stop. Come on. Quit playing."

He smiled at her and then put his arms up behind his head. "You want this dick then get up and take it. Show a nigga who it belongs to. Make this mufucka yours."

"Oh, that ain't a problem, but once I make it mine, my pussy is the only one I better ever smell on it."

Alanee got up and straddled him and then slowly slid down onto his hardness. He brought his hands down and put one on each hip and held onto her as she rode him like a champion horse jockey. It was as if it was the first time for the both of them. Anyone before had been forgotten because it was only the two of them that existed in their world. For hours, it was a fuck fest, and nothing else mattered. Everything they had been through in their lives led up to the moment they became one. When they had finally exhausted themselves, they rested in each other's arms because there was nowhere else in the world either one of them wanted to be.

The morning came upon them quickly, and the ringing of Jarell's cell phone woke them. He didn't want to answer it because he was afraid whoever it was would want to take him from the peace he had finally found in his life. He hit ignore, but not even a minute later, the phone rang again. He finally picked it up and saw that it was his father and knew that he wouldn't stop calling until he answered.

"Sup, Pop? Why you calling me so early?"

"Get outta the pussy and meet me at the spot I used to meet Meek at and don't take all day to get there."

Janahvi hung up before Jarell had a chance to respond. He was trying to spend the whole day beside Alanee but knew that it was too good to be true. His father didn't have urgency in his voice, but for him to call so early did mean it had to be important, so he sat up on the edge of the bed, so he could prepare his mind for whatever he was about to encounter.

Alanee got on her knees behind him and wrapped her arms around his shoulders. He hated to run out and leave her, especially after the wonderful night they had shared together, but he knew not to defy Janahvi Karter, whether he was his father or not.

"Do you really have to go? I was hoping to start the morning out the same way we ended last night."

"Yeah, that was my father, and when he calls, you don't tell him no."

"Do you mind if I ask you a question?"

"Go head, Ma. You ain't gotta ask permission. You can ask me anything."

Alanee wanted to make sure she asked the question right. She didn't want to offend him or make him feel like he wasn't enough for her.

"Jarell, how come you didn't follow in your father's footsteps? I mean, I know that most men want their sons to keep their legacy alive, and if your father is as big of a boss as they say he is, I would think that he would want you to one day take the reins and keep what he's built going strong."

Jarell took a minute to think about what she had asked because he wanted to make sure she understood and respected his answer. He knew that a lot of young, Black brothers had been a product of their environment, and even though he had that same opportunity, he chose to do something different. Something better. He understood that it wasn't just thugs and drug dealers that ended up in prison or a grave, but he felt like his chances were better by choosing not to be one.

"My father started teaching me the rules of the game when I was still a child because he didn't want me to be left behind when the streets called for me. He taught me how to be a killer and a dealer, but to me, that shit wasn't in my dreams, and so I couldn't see it in my future either. My Uncle Meek lost his life while on a drug deal gone wrong while my pops was sitting in a prison cell. I don't want to go out either way, but death and the pen are the only things that living the street life brings. My pops met his father while he was in prison. He lived his whole life not knowing where he came from, so he chose the only thing that accepted him, and that was the hood."

"Oh, my God, so your grandfather was in prison with your father? Where is he now?"

"He died not long after they met. After he explained to my pops why he had been absent his entire life, he could finally rest in peace."

Jarell looked into Alanee's saddened eyes. He felt like she could feel his pain. He brushed a finger over her cheek and continued. "I want to be there to one day have a son and see him grow. Watch him and teach him how to be a man, one that knows how to treat women and knows how to respect boundaries."

"You mean teach him how to be like you?"

"Yeah, I guess so."

"You're going to be a wonderful father one day, Jarell, and I hope that I'm the woman that can give you that blessing."

"Don't worry 'cause you gonna be having me a son and a daughter. You stuck with me now, so I hope you ready for that."

"I've never been more ready for anything in my life, and I'ma give you as many babies as God will allow me to. Some you want and maybe even some you don't expect."

He smiled and bent down to kiss her forehead and then pulled her body to his. He knew that he could spend forever right there with her in his arms, but first, he had to make sure he got rid of anyone who meant to cause her harm. He would risk his life to protect her, and he only hoped that she knew it. He had so many thoughts going through his mind, but he didn't want her to notice, so he continued to play it cool.

"Look, Ma, I hate to do this, but I gotta go. I won't be away from you long. Make sure you ready for some replay action of last night when I get back."

He turned to leave, but she had something else to say. "Jarell, I'm sorry that I've brought so much drama into your peaceful existence. I can tell that your mind and thoughts are going manic, no matter how hard you try to hide it, and I know that I'm to blame."

"Shhh, you don't have anything to be sorry for. You're the reason I have peace and don't ever think anything different. It's other mufuckas that brought the bullshit, and you don't have to worry because I'ma wipe all of them out."

He opened the door and walked out, so he could go meet with his father. Janahvi was an impatient man, and he didn't want to anger him. Jarell had been the reason Bak had been cut off, so he knew that he would come for him and Lanee soon, and he had to make sure he was ready for whatever the nigga brought. He made it down to the parking lot and was about to get in his ride when he heard a noise behind him. He slowly reached for the gun he had tucked down the front of his jeans.

"You don't need that, Jarell. I'm not here to bring you any harm."

After he heard the voice, he turned to face his visitor. "What the hell are you doing creeping up behind me? Don't you think you've caused enough drama in mine and Lanee's life? You ain't even welcome here, so I suggest you turn around and leave."

"Please. I'm not trying to cause any more chaos in Lanee's life. I've done too much damage already, and I know I fucked up, but now, I'm trying to make things right."

"You were supposed to be her best friend, the one person she could depend on the most, but I saw you for who you really were. I tried to tell her not to trust you, but she wouldn't listen. She defended you to the end and look how you repaid her."

"I know, but that wasn't my intention. I just... Lance has always had the best of everything, and I ain't gonna lie. I envied her. She's just so perfect, and everywhere we went, the niggas looked past me, like I wasn't even there. Just to get to her. I only wanted to see how it felt to be in her shoes."

"Yeah? And how did that turn out for you?"

Erica held her head down from the embarrassment she felt. She knew that she had been wrong, and even though she had reconsidered fucking with Bak, in the end, she still went through with it. It had been an unforgivable act and one she couldn't take back. When she lifted her head back up, that was when Jarell noticed the dried blood on the side of her face. He couldn't believe that he had missed it when he first turned around to face her.

"The fuck happened to you?"

"Well, let's just say that things didn't quite turn out the way I had hoped, and now, I feel like shit. I don't know. I happened to walk in on Bak and Brightman talking. They didn't know that I was there, listening at first, and I heard them talking about going after you and your father, and then, Bak is supposed to eliminate me. I confronted him, and he pulled a gun on me, but when he pulled the trigger, it didn't go off, so he hit me in the head with the butt of it. I think that he thought he had killed me because he covered me with a blanket and then ran out. I knew that I had to get away before he got back and realized I was still alive."

Erica took a short breath and then continued. "I really wanted to believe that he gave a fuck about me, but he was only using me to piss Lanee off. I feel bad about telling her all that stuff about you. I know it wasn't my place to do so, but he left me no choice. That bastard has to pay for all he's done."

"Where that nigga at now?"

"I don't know. He got a phone call and rushed out after he covered up my body. As soon as I heard his car drive away, I got out of there, and I haven't looked back."

Jarell looked into Erica's frightened eyes and knew that she was telling the truth, but he was still skeptical about the situation. He thought for a minute about what he should do and finally pulled out his cell phone and dialed. Erica wasn't sure who he was calling, but when he revealed that information, she breathed a sigh of relief.

"Lanee, baby, don't ask me no questions right now. I need you to open the door and let Erica in. She's on her way up."

He hung up without waiting for a response because he didn't think it would be a good one. He knew for sure that

Alanee wouldn't go against what he said because she was too loyal to do such a thing. She respected anything he asked of her, and that was one of the reasons he loved her so much. He felt better knowing that someone would be there with her because he didn't know what Bak's next move would be.

"Go on up. Lanee's gonna have the door open for you but don't try no stupid shit because I can assure you that whatever Bak had planned for you ain't nothing compared to what you gonna get from me if something happens to her because of you."

"I understand, Jarell, but I'm not gonna do anything or say anything else to hurt her. I give you my word."

"Aiight then. I gotta go handle some shit, but I'll be back."

Jarell turned around and got in his ride, but he didn't pull off until Erica was in the elevator and on her way up to his penthouse. He knew that he would kill her with his bare hands if something happened to Alanee. He'd be damned if he let anyone steal the happiness he had finally found. He knew deep in his gut that he was about to be part of a war, one that he was determined to win. He wished there was a way to keep his father out of it, but he knew Janahvi wouldn't let him fight alone. Him and Alanee were living the life that his parents did, and theirs was a love worth fighting for. Jarell felt like his and Alanee's was too, and he would fight with all he had inside of him. M'Baku Reynolds wasn't ready for the wrath Jarell would unleash on him, and he couldn't wait til Bak could feel his pain.

Chapter Fifteen

Trameeka and Brightman sat and stared at one another while they waited on Bak to meet them. Neither one could stand the other, but a truce had to be called in order for the plan Bak had made to work. Brightman pulled on the blunt he held between his fingers while Trameeka picked up her phone and focused her sight on other things she would rather look at.

"The fuck you over there texting?"

"None of your damn business and who the hell are you to question me?"

Brightman took another pull off his blunt and closed his eyes in pleasure when he exhaled the smoke. The weed was strong and had him in a zone, but the bitch that sat across from him had blown his high. He had never trusted her and wasn't about to start. He would never allow a bitch to pussy whip him the way that she had done his boy. Bak was blinded by a quick nut because Brightman couldn't believe that he had included her in their plan to take over the entire city by robbing her Uncle Nahvi, the biggest drug lord in the state. He refused to believe that she would really go against her cousin and uncle in the end. Brightman quickly became paranoid and picked up his four five, which had been sitting on the couch beside him. He held it tightly in his grip and put his eyes back on Trameeka.

"You must think I'm a dumb mufucka to believe that you down with putting your people out of business."

The comment had been unexpected, and it threw her completely off. She stopped typing the text and looked up from her phone. She saw the cold steel that he held in his hand, but little did he know, she had some fire power of her own, and she wasn't afraid to use it. She lived for moments like that to come along, so she could show a bitch what she was made of. She sat her phone down and leaned forward, placing her arms on her slightly parted thighs. She looked up and made sure to make eye contact before she spoke.

"You are a dumb motherfucker if you think that piece you are holding in your hand scares me. Do you know where the hell I came from? Huh? I was produced by the realest and thoroughest nigga ever made, and I was born to carry on the legacy he left behind. So don't fucking think that you and that little gun you're holding is enough to intimidate a bitch like me."

"This ain't no intimidation tactic. I'm just trying to figure out what you're really up to."

"And just what are you talking about, Brightman? You talking about the run that's planned on my uncle? The one that I"m going to lead?"

"Yeah. That's exactly what I'm talking about. That's 'pose to be your family, but you claim you willing to go against them for a nigga like Bak, a nigga that passes out community dick and is doing all this to get his ex-bitch back. I'm just wondering how it will all play out. Who you really gonna be loyal to in the end?"

Trameeka thought about what he had asked. Brightman was too smart for his own good sometimes, but she was the wrong bitch to question.

"I'm going to be loyal to myself in the end because when this is all over, I'm going to be on top. You see, what you don't seem to understand about me is the fact that I don't claim dick, no matter how much I enjoy a good ride. Besides, I'm not going against my family just to benefit Bak. I'm doing it for my own selfish needs. Needs that you know absolutely nothing about. I don't give a damn about his ex-bitch. He can run off into the sunset with her for all I care. I can get good dick anywhere and from anyone I choose. Even you."

Trameeka was a cocky bitch, and that was one of the reasons Brightman couldn't stand her ass.

"Nah, your ass ain't classy enough to sit on this beast. Besides, I don't fuck behind my niggas. I live up to the code, and a bitch like you ain't gonna change that."

"Yeah? Whatever. I got some shit I need to go handle but tell Bak I'll be back through."

"Oh, so you ain't gonna wait? You know he gonna be pissed about you not being here when he gets here, and I don't wanna hear that shit."

"Oh, well, looks like that's your problem, not mine."

Trameeka walked out and slammed the door behind her. Brightman truly felt like she was up to no good, and he wished that he could prove it. She had held tight to the fact that Janahvi Karter was her uncle, and he could only wonder what else she had kept hidden. She was a true gangsta bitch and knew what loyalty meant to the game, so he wanted to know what had made her so bitter and angry enough to turn against her own people. The question he wanted to ask was would she really be going against them, or was it all just a set up?

He had hoped to ask the right question and trip her up. She was a female, and no matter how gangsta one was, they still had a soft side. He wanted to make her slip and reveal her true intentions, but he saw that she had too much sense to do so. He was looking for a reason to smoke her ass. Bak was too sweet on her to see her for who she really was, but he didn't give a fuck about her, so he decided to look out for his boy like he had always done. Bak was blinded by pussy, and Brightman feared that one day, it would be the death of his friend.

He wondered where she had to run off to so quickly and had thought about jumping in his ride and following her but then decided that he didn't have time to chase after a bitch. He would sit back and wait for Bak to get there, and while he waited, he began to form his own plan. Trameeka had to go, and he would rid the Earth of her by any means necessary, and he'd be damned if he let Bak or anyone else stand in his way.

Chapter Sixteen

Alanee unlocked the door and opened it for Erica like she was told to do. She wondered why she had shown up there and couldn't believe that Jarell would allow the bitch anywhere in their vicinity, and he better have a good excuse for doing so. She truly wanted to believe Erica when she told her she felt bad for the shit she pulled with Bak, but after she told her all that stuff about Jarell, she knew better. If Erica cared anything about her or felt bad for anything she had done, she never would have brought any more drama to her.

As soon as Erica appeared, Alanee rolled her eyes and walked away, leaving the door wide open for her to enter. She felt like she didn't owe her any hospitality, and she wasn't about to be fake. She went into the bedroom that she shared with Jarell and slammed the door behind her. She had no interest in listening to anything Erica had to say because to her, it was all bullshit.

"Come on, Lanee. Damn. I know that I shouldn't have come here and told you all that stuff, whether it was true or not. I'm sorry, and I'm here now to try and make it right."

Alanee didn't want to be anywhere close to Erica, so she hollered through the bedroom door. It made her sick to her stomach to think of Erica's betrayal when she had been someone she thought she could trust.

"Fuck you, Erica. I don't want to hear shit you got to say. I don't know why the hell Jarell let your flaw ass come up here anyway because you don't mean either one of us any good. Jarell let you up here so sit your ass out there and wait for him to get back. And don't try to fuck him like you did Bak."

"Wow, Lanee, I'm not here on no bullshit this time. Please come out. I swear I'm done. Bak is a piece of shit, and I only came over here so I could warn Jarell and tell him the plans that Bak and Brightman have made to take Janahvi Karter out."

As soon as Alanee heard Janahvi's name, she jumped up out of the bed. She wouldn't be able to live with herself if something happened to Jarell's father because of her. If she had to leave Jarell alone and be with Bak to protect them, she would, no matter how much it disgusted her. She would do whatever she had to do. She slowly opened the bedroom door and walked out to face her frenemy. She wanted to look her in the eyes while she listened to what she had to say, but as soon as she was close enough, she saw the dried blood and ran to her aid.

"Oh, my God, Erica, what happened? Who did this to you?"

"Bak did it. He hit me with the butt of the gun after he tried to shoot me, and the gun jammed."

Alanee pulled Erica into her arms and then walked her to the bathroom, so she could help her clean up. She couldn't believe that Bak had gone crazy enough to try and kill Erica, and it scared her to think of what else he might do to get her back.

"Come on and let's get you cleaned up. Why did he do this to you?"

"I walked in on him and Brighman making plans and threatened to tell you everything. He wanted to kill me, Lanee, but for some reason, the gun jammed, and I was spared, but if he would have been able to take my life, it was only because I deserved it."

"No, Erica, it's okay. You don't deserve to die, no matter what you've done, so don't say that. I've forgiven you for everything, and I would hate myself if something happened to you."

"Oh, Lanee, how could you ever care about me right now? I was supposed to have your back at all costs, and yet, I stabbed you in the heart. I don't deserve a friend like you, and if you never forgave me, I wouldn't even be mad."

"No, don't say stuff like that. We done been through so much together, and we made a pact that we would never allow a man to come between us. We're going to stick to that. Besides, look what I got out of it. I now have a good man, who really and truly cares about me. I can lie in my bed in peace at night, even when he is away, and know that he's not with another bitch. I'm at peace, Erica, and it's all because of you."

The two friends shared a hug, and then, Alanee finished helping Erica get cleaned up. When she had washed all the blood from her hair and face, she looked up at Alanee and smiled.

"Thank you for forgiving me, Lanee. I swear I will never do anything to hurt you again."

Alanee felt like Erica had really learned her lesson, and she hoped that their friendship could get back on track, the way that it had been before the betrayal. When they walked out of the bathroom, Alanee went to her closet and pulled out a Victoria's Secret sweatsuit and gave it to Erica to put on and then left her in the room to get dressed. Erica looked around the room and admired its beauty. She felt like she belonged in that world of white custom sofas, trendy throw pillows, and marble statues, but she knew that it was something she could never afford, and her hopes of landing a baller didn't seem so promising anymore.

After she got dressed, she slid on the pair of house slippers Alanee had laid at her feet and walked out to see what her friend was up to. She could hear voices coming from the kitchen and figured that Jarell had made it back, so that was where she headed. She wanted to tell him and Alanee everything so that they would be prepared for whatever Bak came at them with. When she got closer to the kitchen, she stopped in her tracks and listened. The voice gave her chills, and she was scared to take another step. She couldn't believe that Bak had the nerve to show up there and wondered if he knew that she was there too. She was thankful that she still had her cell phone and pulled it out, so she could record the exchange between him and Alanee.

"So, you up in this big ass penthouse suite with a nigga like you been fucking him a long ass time. Tell me, Lanee, was his ass dipping in my pussy while you was still playing house with me?"

"No, Bak, I was true to you, but you couldn't give me the same courtesy. You fathered a fucking child with another bitch and passed his little ass off like he belonged to your boy, and then, you turn around and fuck my best friend. You are a true piece of shit, and you deserve whatever karma comes your way."

"Oh, yeah. That's how your ass feels after all the shit I done did for you? Bitch, for five years, I made sure your ass lived in the lap of luxury. You ain't want for shit, and yet you still disrespect me by running off in the wind with the next nigga."

"You told me to leave, remember? I begged you not to kick me out, but my words didn't mean a damn thing to you, so you can take that five years of bullshit and shove it up your ass."

"Oh, you think 'cause this nigga got you in a high rise that you can talk to me any kind of way. I'm still running shit, Lanee, and you still belong to me, so you might as well suck it up and let's get out of here."

Alanee couldn't believe that he would actually think she wanted to go anywhere with him, but then, she remembered his plans for Janahvi Karter and tried to cut him a deal. "If I go with you, will you call off the hit on Jarell's father? He has done nothing to you, so why are you going after him anyway?"

"You wanna know why? Because your little boyfriend had his old man cut off my dope supply and left me out in the cold. Mufucka should have just stayed in his place and kept waiting them tables. So, since he felt the need to take my bitch and my money, it's only right that I pay him back. But I'll tell you what. I'll make Brightman go easy on him, just for you."

"No, Bak. Please call it off and I'll leave with you right now, and we can spend the rest of our lives together. We never have to look back. It will be just me and you. I mean, you have to know that I still love you, and I can't lie, I miss what we shared."

Erica was thrown off by what Alanee said, but she knew her best friend as well as she knew herself. She knew that Alanee was saying what she needed to say to get Bak to pull out of his plans. She trusted that Alanee knew what she was doing, but she didn't trust that Bak would hold to his end of the bargain. She didn't want things to backfire on her friend in the end. She decided to make her presence known, but what she heard next stopped her.

"Look, Lanee, I only fucked that grimy bitch, Erica, to piss you off, but you know her ass didn't mean shit to me. She actually had the nerve to think I was gonna wife her, but she's a bottom feeder, and I'd slit my own throat before I'd put a ring on her finger. But thanks to me, neither one of us have to worry about her again."

"What are you talking about, Bak? You were wrong as hell, and you know it. That was my best friend, and she was like a sister to me. I should have seen it coming though because I caught her so many times, watching you, and I knew I should have called her on it. That bitch always been jealous of me, and she always will be. She violated the friend code, and there ain't no coming back from that. But I do know she better not ever fix her mouth to call and tell me how sorry she is. What she did to me was unforgivable."

"Oh, don't worry, Lanee. Her ass is no longer in a position to call you because I axed that bitch. That hoe dead as fuck."

"What are you saying, Bak? Are you telling me you killed her for real?"

"That's exactly what I'm saying. That bitch is laid up, leaking from the dome, as we speak."

"That's good for her ass because if she would have showed up at my door, I was gonna beat that ass for the old and the new. I guess I'm gonna have to reward you for saving me the trouble."

"Hmmm. Well, why don't you go head and let a nigga get a little hit of that pussy before we get out of here? My dick hard as a rock, just thinking about fucking you in that chump's bed."

"And what you gonna do if he walks in and catches us?"

"I'ma skeet on that mufucka."

The two of them shared a laugh, and then, Alanee walked up closer to him, so she could plant a kiss on his lips. It made her sick on her stomach to do it, but she had to think quickly. She needed to get him out of the penthouse before he realized Erica was in the next room. If he found out, it could end very badly for both of them.

"Come on, Bak, take me home so we can make up for old time's sake."

"Baby, you ain't said nothing but a word. Let's get out of here."

Erica wasn't sure what to do after they left, so she paced the floor until she could think of something. She wished that she had Jarell's number, so she could call him, but since she didn't, she would just have to wait until he showed back up. She couldn't lie. She was scared as hell because she didn't know what would happen once Bak found her gone. He thought that he had killed her, but Erica refused to die. She was so worried about Alanee that she began to bite her nails to the white meat. It had been a long time since she had indulged in the nervous habit, but she couldn't think of anything else to do.

She finally sat down and began to take in her surroundings. The decor of the place was immaculate and a far cry from what she was used to. The small, rundown apartment she lived in with her mother was atrocious compared to the penthouse. She had been used to looking at water-stained ceilings, ripped wallpaper, mismatched furniture, and a rust stained sink that stayed full of dirty dishes. She couldn't hear voices and TV noises coming through Jarell's walls. It was as if his penthouse was in a world of its own. She could only imagine how it would feel to fall asleep without hearing the sounds of drive-by shootings or mice scurrying in the thin walls. She deserved to live like a queen too, but she had yet to find her king and started to feel like she never would.

Erica had finally calmed down enough to lie down on the plush sofa. She pulled the blanket that hung over the back of it onto her small body. She was too afraid to turn the television on, so she laid in the silence of the room. The clean smell of air freshening products tickled her nose and brought her some peace. It had been a long time since she had turned to God for anything, but she took the time to send a short prayer up to him for her friend, and then, she closed her eyes and fell right to sleep.

Erica slept so peacefully and so deeply that she didn't even hear the door when it opened. The intruder walked in and stood over her in an intimidating stance. They didn't want to disturb her, at least not yet, so instead, they sat in the chair across from her. They would wait until she woke up and then, they would get the answers they'd come for.

Chapter Seventeen

The strong smell of gunpowder stung Jarell in the nose as soon as he walked into the lobby of the shooting range his father owned. It had been a while since he'd been there, but the place was still as familiar as ever. The racks of guns that hung on the wall seemed to have increased in numbers since his last visit. So many different makes and models but all with the same ill effect. Each one of them had the power to take the lives of not only one's enemies but also their friends, and no matter how hard the politicians tried, they could never completely ban them.

The heft of a weapon in one's hand, and the sense of calm as one steadied their breathing to take a shot, made a mufucka feel like they could run the world. Jarell could still remember the first time his father took him there. The first bullet that left the barrel of the gun caused a painful jerk of pressure in his shoulder, but he refused to let that stop him. Each shot became easier, and before long, it was as natural to him as breathing. He loved the feel of a weapon being held in his hands and the tingling rush of adrenaline from firing it. It had been a while since he had to push a nigga's wig back, and the thought of doing so made his dick hard.

He made his way to the bulletproof glass encased office where his father sat and waited for him. Janahvi Karter sat in a plush swivel chair, smoking on a Cuban cigar. It was the only place he would smoke one at because Ashley couldn't stand the smell of it. As soon as Jarell walked in, Janahvi opened the crystal case and offered one to him, even though he knew he would turn it down.

"Have a seat, son. We have some things to discuss."

"Nah, I think I'll stand. Besides, I'm not planning on sticking around long. I need to get back to Lanee."

Janahvi cut his eyes up to Jarell and then sat the cigar in the ashtray. "You will sit down, and you will stay until I'm done saying what I have to say."

The authority in Janahvi's voice spoke volumes to his only son, and Jarell knew not to defy him. He looked his father in the eyes and took the seat across from him. "Aiight, Pops, you have my full attention."

"Very well. You understand that we have a problem on our hands because of this girl you have brought into your life."

"Don't worry. I'm going to handle the problem before it makes its way. It's my issue, and I'll deal with it."

"No, son, it's our issue. Anything that affects you does the same to me, and anytime a problem arises, we have to become one. I would never allow you to fight alone, even if I knew you would win. You know that I would give my last breath for you, but what I need to know is if this girl is worth it."

"You damn right she's worth it. What kind of question is that to ask? I'm in love with her, Pops, and I ain't trying to imagine my life without her."

"But does she feel the same way that you do? If a better offer came along, would she jump at it?"

"The fuck you mean by that?"

"You came to me, and you asked me to cut off the nigga, but I'm wondering why? You already had the girl, so what did cutting him off prove? Kinda makes me feel like it was an insurance plan to keep her from going back to him and if that's what it was, then maybe you need to let her go. What made her run to you? Your status or just your handsome face?"

"Lanee ain't like that, Pops. She didn't even know I owned the restaurant or what my last name represented. She found that out only recently. She left that fuck nigga because he ain't treat her right, and even if that mufucka turned millionaire overnight, she would never go back to him."

Janahvi sat back and lit the cigar once again. He didn't mind going to war and fighting, but he just needed to make sure the cause was worth fighting for. He stared Jarell in the eyes and saw that same hunger he used to have in his. His son was ready to lay down his life for a woman he felt was right for him, and who was Janahvi to judge him? When Janahvi sat back up, he put the cigar in the ashtray once again and folded his hands together.

"I have one more thing to tell you, and I can assure you that you are not going to like it."

Jarell nodded his head, as if to tell his father that he was ready to hear it, but he didn't expect what came out of his father's mouth. "Trameeka has joined M'Baku and his boy, Brightman, in a fight against my camp."

"What? Nah, Pops, don't play with me like that. Meeka would never do no shit like that. She too loyal to the cause."

"Yeah, I thought so too, but she called me earlier. She asked me to give Bak a spot on my team and not a low spot. She wants him to take the seat that you should have sat in long ago."

"And if you don't do what she's asked, what happens?"

"She takes him to all the hot spots and runs in, taking whatever is there. Everyone is familiar with her, so they won't hesitate to give her what she asks them for."

"Nah, she wouldn't do that to you. Ain't no mufuckin way she'd do that shit. I'ma go over there and see her right now, so I can find out what her fuckin problem is."

Jarell stood angrily from his seat, but Janahvi lifted a hand and pointed a finger to the chair his son had risen from. No one moved without his say so, and Jarell knew that, so for him to get up as if he ran shit made Janahvi feel disrespected. Jarell read his father's expression and knew what he was telling him and then sat back down to hear what he had to say.

"Her problem is you. I guess she didn't like the fact that you went over there and checked her about something she didn't do. You tested her loyalty without even giving her a chance to explain. I will tell you this so make sure you listen good. Trameeka is the daughter of the most loyal nigga I ever met, and she carries those same traits that Meek did. The information about you and my business didn't come from her. It came from Brightman."

"How the fuck that nigga know all our shit?"

"Not only is he very smart and pays attention, somehow, he got involved with one of my runners, and she fell weak. At first, he didn't know who he was involved with, but your name happened to be mentioned in a conversation, and she overheard it. When he found out she was familiar with you, he convinced her to tell everything."

"Where the hell is the bitch at now?"

"Oh, you don't have to worry about her because her time on Earth expired real quick. Ya know not all women are as strong as your mother, and if you can't find one that is like her, you need to walk away."

"Don't worry, Dad, Lanee is far from weak and I trust that she would hold me down if it came to that."

"For all our sake, I hope you're right. You can go now. I'll call you when it's time to make a move."

Jarell stood again and was about to say something else but thought better of it. He opened the door and walked out, but instead of leaving, he decided to let off a few rounds. He stopped outside and went to lane twelve. It was one that his father would have a clear view of, and he wanted him to see that he was ready for whatever came his way. He pushed the button, which made his target move away from him. When it was a nice distance, he pulled his piece out of the waist of his jeans and fired. Once he emptied the clip, he pushed the button again and made the target come close. He admired the nine holes he had put in the bullseye and then turned to look his father in the eyes. Janahvi nodded his head in acceptance and then closed the blinds on the window. Jarell shook his head and smiled because no matter how hard his father acted, he knew he had a soft spot for him. Even when Janahvi said nothing at all, Jarell knew what he was thinking. His father was proud of him, and all Jarell wanted to do was keep it that way.

Jarell got in his ride and started the engine but didn't pull off. He sat there and thought about all his father had said. He didn't want to second guess Lanee's loyalty to him, but he had to remember that she had spent five, long years loving another man before him. Was she really all the way done with M'Baku Reynolds, or had she been playing on Jarell's emotions for the short time they had been together? He knew what it would mean if he found out it was all a lie because it would be him that would have to kill her, and he wasn't sure that he would be up to the task.

He finally put the car in gear and drove home, so he could ask Lanee things he needed to know. He wanted to look her in the eyes, so he could tell if she was telling the truth or not. He pulled into the parking garage and eased into his spot. He looked around and listened closely because something felt off. He reloaded the clip on his weapon and slowly stepped out of the vehicle. He observed the rows of cars and trucks parked in their assigned spaces and shook his head. The talk he had with his father had made him paranoid, but he shook it off and got on the elevator that would lead him to the love he hoped was real.

When he opened the front door, the place seemed too quiet and also unfamiliar. He felt like he should have heard some type of movement or at least a conversation going on since he had sent Erica up to sit with Lanee until he got back. He checked all the rooms of the penthouse and became worried when he found that Lanee wasn't there. He pulled his cell phone out of his pocket and was about to call her when he noticed a figure lying on the couch, but it wasn't Lanee. He sat down in the chair across from her and waited.

His wait wasn't long because it was as if Erica felt him watching her. She opened her eyes slowly, and once she saw that it was Jarell, she felt a sense of calmness.

"Jarell, you startled me. When did you get back?"

"Where the fuck is Lanee at and don't lie?"

Erica sat up and planted her feet on the thick carpet. She stood and was about to walk away, but Jarell stood too and stopped her.

"I asked you a question, and you ain't going nowhere until you answer it."

Erica looked down and then sat back on the couch before she answered him.

"She left with Bak. I tried to talk her out of it, but I guess seeing him made her realize she missed him more than she thought."

"The fuck you mean? I don't believe that shit for a second, so you need to come better than that."

"I'm telling you the truth, Jarell. The only reason she called you that night was because she knew it would eat Bak up inside, knowing she ran to the next man. He never would have thought she had someone else she could call on, so he didn't think anything of it when he made her leave."

"Yeah, and you just couldn't wait to step in and take her place."

"That wasn't supposed to happen, but when Bak touched me, I couldn't resist him. It had been so long since I had a good fuck, and I just wanted to see exactly what had Lanee hooked. I regretted it after I did it, but I can't change it now. Besides, Lanee is a better fit for him than I am because I ain't about to bow down to a nigga that pushes his dick up in every chick he meets."

"So, you saying she went with him willingly?"

"Yeah, I hate that she left me here to tell you the bad news, but you needed to know."

Jarell suddenly remembered what Erica had told him when he first encountered her in the parking garage. He wondered how Bak felt when he saw that she was still alive, so he asked her.

"So, that nigga ain't feel no type of way when he came up in my shit and saw that you still breathing?"

"Honestly, he didn't even know I was here. When Lanee looked out the peephole and saw him, she hid me out in the other room. I gotta admit that bitch had my back, even after all I put her through. I overheard them talking, and Bak said that if she gave him one more chance, he would keep it real with her, and of course she fell for it. When she snuck back in the room and told me she was leaving with him, I told her she was making a mistake, but she said she wanted to be with him. I'm so sorry, Jarell. You just gonna have to move on without her."

For some reason, Jarell didn't believe her. There was no way Alanee would run back to the nigga who treated her like shit. She was a woman who demanded to be respected, and she would settle for nothing less. If he knew her like he thought he did then he would say that she only left with him to protect Erica because if he would have found out she was still alive, it could have turned out badly for both of them.

"Where did he take her to?"

"Jarell, I know you don't want to believe me, but I'm being serious. Lanee chose to go with Bak. She had told me how much she wished that he would change, and if he did, she would go back to him. Somehow, he put it in her mind that he was a different man and that he had learned from his mistakes. But don't worry about her. Let him have her. She wasn't right for you anyway."

"Oh, yeah, that's what you think? Because from what I understand, you were pushing mighty hard for her to leave that nigga."

"That's only because I thought I wanted to be with him, but he's not the man I want."

Erica pulled off the t-shirt she wore and walked closer to Jarell. Her nipples hardened as soon as the cool air hit them. Her breasts were larger than Lanee's but not nearly as beautiful. Maybe it was because of her personality. She was a pretty girl, but as soon as she opened her mouth, she killed the vibe. She was playing herself out and didn't even know it, but Jarell decided to bring her back down to size and gave her a reality check.

"That shit you standing here, trying to pull, ain't gonna work on me because a piece of pussy don't make me the way it does the next nigga. Unlike Bak, I would never stab Lanee in the heart, and you, your sex appeal is just like your personality, dead as a mufucka, so put your shit back on and get the hell outta my space."

Erica was so embarrassed because no man had ever cut her so deep, not even Bak. She knew that once Jarell told Alanee about the incident, she would never be able to fix it. She had fucked up, but it was too late to turn back and change what she had done. She grabbed the t-shirt she had taken off, put it back on, and sat back down because she didn't know what else to do, but then, she figured she might as well tell the truth.

"Jarell, I'm sorry. Everything I just told you was a lie, except for the fact that Lanee went willingly, but she only did it to protect me. If Bak would have known that I was here, he would have killed me for real and possibly even her. She would never go back to him for any other reason. She really loves you, and I'm sure she's expecting you to come for her, so please don't let her down."

"So, she did what she did to protect you, and you pay her back by trying to fuck me? I don't know what kind of friend you claim to be, but I do know that you're the kind that Lanee doesn't need in her life. Why don't you do us all a favor and disappear because if I ever see your face again, I might just kill you myself."

Erica knew that he meant every word. She thought about having to go back home to where she lived with her mother, and the thought was disappointing. She didn't want to live like that anymore, but what else could she do? Why couldn't she find someone who wanted to give her the kind of life that Alanee had? Wasn't she deserving of having everything too? She decided to pour her heart out and hoped Jarell would listen and understand.

"Jarell, I know that I haven't been the best friend to Lanee, but I truly do love and care for her. I've had it rough my whole life, and I ain't never had shit. I live with my mom in a rundown apartment and wear knock offs that I find in thrift stores, just to try and blend in, but nothing I could ever do would stack up to Lanee."

"Then maybe you should try just being yourself. You never know what you may find when you start focusing on you instead of someone else. You've made mistakes, Erica, and that means you're human, but it's never too late to correct them. When you get your mind right, you may very well come out on top without pushing someone else down to get there."

"Thanks, I really need to hear that, and just so you know, I'm glad Lanee has someone in her life like you because she deserves it."

Erica stood to leave because she felt like she had worn out her welcome long enough. She wasn't sure where she was going, but it definitely wouldn't be backwards. She opened the door to walk out, but the sound of Jarell's voice stopped her.

"Here, take this and go somewhere and try to rebuild your life. Do something better with what you have and make your own path. There's someone out there meant just for you, and when they come along, you won't have to go through any changes to be with them because they're gonna love you for you."

Erica took the small duffel bag Jarell handed her and opened it. When she saw it was full of hundred-dollar bills, she was speechless. She had never seen so much money in her life, and she vowed to spend it wisely. She quickly closed the bag up, as if the money would disappear if she didn't. She smiled and gave Jarell a hug and walked away, hoping to leave the past behind.

Jarell closed the door and walked to his bookshelf. He pulled out the book, *The 48 Laws of Power*, by Robert Green. When the bookshelf slid from the wall, he smiled as he looked up at his array of weapons. He slowly and meticulously picked out his favorites. He was about to put something hot in M'Baku Reynolds's ass and take back what was rightfully his.

Chapter Eighteen

"How dare you bring this bitch up in my shit? I don't know who the hell you take me for, Bak, but you got the wrong one. You better take her ass to Gina's."

"Damn, Meeka, why you trippin like that? I thought you ain't care who I had on the side as long as you straight. Why the sudden change?"

"Ain't no sudden change, so miss me with that bullshit, but you ain't gonna disrespect me in my own home. Now, you can take your bitch and go elsewhere."

Bak could not believe that Trameeka was tripping on him about Alanee. He had always taken her for a hard bitch, who didn't give a damn about the next female, but he realized he had been wrong. He was afraid to take Alanee anywhere else because he believed she would dip on him. He wasn't convinced that she had gone with him because she missed him, so he wondered what the real reason was. He knew that Jarell would never think to check his cousin's house for Alanee, especially with the beef he had going on with Trameeka herself. Bak wanted to use Alanee as leverage, but he had to convince Trameeka that it was a good idea.

"Aye, let me holla at you in the bedroom real quick."

Trameeka looked at Alanee and rolled her eyes and then turned to do as Bak said. Once they were in the bedroom, she folded her arms over her chest and demanded to know what he had up his sleeve.

"Alright, Bak, you got five minutes to tell me what is up, and if I don't like what you got to say, you and your bitch are getting up outta my shit."

"Damn, Meeka, you don't cut a nigga no kind of slack."

"Yeah, well, that's because you and no one else is going to take advantage of me. Now you need to start talking because you've already wasted a minute."

"Alright. Alright, damn. I brought Lanee here, so we could use her as a type of leverage, just in case your cousin don't wanna sit his ass down and take what we giving him."

"Yeah, that's what you claiming, but I feel like your ass is lying. You really expect me to believe that she's not with you for your own personal pleasure?"

"Meeka, come on. I give you my word. I'm with you, baby. We gonna stick to the plan and run up in those mufuckin houses and take what we can get, but when it's time to get to the big dog, we gonna need something to bargain with. You think Jarell is going to let Alanee be a sacrifice? Hell no. He gonna do whatever it takes to protect her."

"You really think my Uncle Nahvi gives a damn about her ass? Hell no. She ain't gonna do us no good, no matter how much my cousin loves her. Uncle Nahvi ain't gonna risk his life or Aunt Ashley's life for a bitch they don't even know that well."

Alanee stood from the couch and crept to the door of the bedroom, so she could listen to the exchange between Bak and Trameeka. She knew that Bak had bad intentions when he came for her, but she had to leave with him in order to save Erica. She reached for her cell phone, which she usually kept in her back pocket, and when it wasn't there, she remembered that she had left it on the bathroom counter when she was helping Erica get cleaned up. She turned and saw Bak's cell phone on the end table by the couch and grabbed it and then ran out of the house. Meanwhile, Bak and Trameeka continued to argue about her presence.

"So, you don't think Jarell's father gives a damn about his feelings."

"Bak, I know you're smarter than that. I mean, Jarell can find another woman to be with. Before he lets something happen to his parents, he will let Lanee fall. Now, get the bitch outta my shit. I won't tell you again."

"And if I don't, what you gonna do about it?"

"I'ma let you run in those houses without me, and I can assure you when that happens, you won't be coming back out. I'm your only hope of coming up the way you want, so I suggest you stick with me."

"And what exactly am I supposed to do with her?"

"I don't give a damn what you do, but your time is up."

Trameeka opened the door and walked out of the room with Bak hot on her trail. She smiled when she walked into the living room and found that Alanee had left, but Bak was pissed, and when he noticed that she had taken his phone, he became angrier.

"I'ma kill that bitch as soon as I find her, but right now, we got a plan to carry out so let's go."

"Okay but give me a minute to change. If you want this to work, you gotta let me dress the part."

Bak gave her a crazy look but knew that she was right. Trameeka had planned to walk up in the stash houses and tell the workers that Janahvi had sent her to pick up the money and whatever dope they had left. All of the workers were familiar with her, so it should have been an easy job. Bak couldn't wait to have all that money and product at his disposal. He just hoped that everything went according to the plans he had made. He appreciated the fact that he had the power to make Trameeka turn against her own people. When it was all said and done, he would get rid of her too. She just didn't know it yet. He didn't need a disloyal bitch on his side because if it was that easy to turn her against her family, she could one day be convinced to turn on him too.

The thought of having the entire city under his reign had his dick on swole. He figured they had a couple of more hours they could kill and still stick to the plan, so he walked back into the bedroom where Trameeka stood, wearing only a black lace thong. Her fat ass was perfect, and all he wanted to do was spread it and slide inside her wet pussy from the back. He had to admit he was damn sure gonna miss her because he hadn't met a bitch yet that could suck his dick the way that she did.

He walked up behind her and without saying a word, put his arm around her from the back. He slid a hand down the front of the thongs and pushed a finger into her wetness. He knew that she wouldn't try to stop him because their sex was the best thing about what they shared together. Trameeka grinded on his finger but only for a minute because she needed something more to fill her up. She thought to herself that she might as well get in one more good orgasm before the mission at hand. She turned around to face him and immediately reached for his manhood. It was a shame that all that good meat was going to go to waste, but she would enjoy it while it was available.

"You gonna just stand here and play in this pussy, or you gonna bend me over and fuck me right?"

Bak loved Trameeka's boldness. It was what had attracted him to her the first time they met. He remembered it as if it was yesterday. He pulled up on the block with Brightman and saw her outside a stash house with the fellas. He was about to ask one of the boys who she was, but she saved him the trouble and introduced herself.

"What's up, playa? My name is Trameeka, and I bet you could lay down some good dick."

"Wow, you sure know how to call a man out, but I'm cool with it because you ain't said nothing but a word."

That night, Trameeka and Bak fucked for hours and never looked back. Their sex game had been off the charts, and neither expected anything more. They had an understanding from the jump that there would be no strings attached, and they had stuck to their word to that day.

Trameeka walked to the bed and positioned herself doggystyle. It was her favorite way to get fucked because she loved the roughness of it, and Bak didn't mind giving it to her gangsta. He slid inside of her with ease, and with each thrust, he went harder and stronger. He admired how her wetness covered the length of his dick and the way she talked shit with every thrust.

"Yeah, Bak. Nigga, give me that dick. This your pussy, baby, and don't you ever forget it."

He could feel himself on the verge of a nut, and even though he usually pulled out, he decided to empty his nut sack inside of her. He wasn't worried about getting her pregnant because he didn't plan on letting her live long enough to carry a child. He planned on eliminating her as soon as their mission was accomplished. And once he had her and Jarell six feet deep in the earth, he would get Alanee back on his good side.

After he came, him and Trameeka washed off and got ready for their first mission. He would meet up with Brightman afterwards and make plans to get rid of Erica's body. He was certain that it was still safe under the blanket he had covered it with. He had asked Brightman to take care of it for him, but he said it wasn't his kill, so it wasn't his issue, but he would help him when he was ready.

After him and Trameeka were dressed, he went out to the black Range Rover she had purchased for the mission. He decided that when it was all over, he would burn her body inside of it. The thought brought a smile to his face, and when Trameeka got in the driver seat beside him, she wanted to know what he was smiling about.

"What you so happy about? We gearing up to go on a death mission if things don't go right, and you sitting up in this ride smiling. You save that for when it's over."

"Nah, sweet thang, I feel like everything is going to go as planned. Shit, I'm with the right bitch, and ain't no way anything could go wrong as long as you leading the way."

"Mmm hmm. Sucking up is not a good look for you, but I'll take the compliment."

Trameeka started the Range and drove to the rec center across town. She saw the young boys from the projects playing basketball on the outdoor court. She thought about how they could be out on the blocks selling dope, but the rec center gave them other options. However, the rec center had only been a cover up for the real operation, and she knew that she would have the least amount of trouble if she robbed the men who ran it. It wasn't one of her Uncle Nahvi's establishments, so she knew she needed to be careful, even though she had already set it up.

"The fuck is we doing at a rec center? I ain't trying to play no damn basketball."

"Bak, just chill out. My uncle owns this spot, and this is where he keeps most of his drugs. I figured that we might as well start off big and work our way down the line, so if something goes in another direction, we will have at least got the big stuff."

"Ya know what? That's why I fucks with you."

Trameeka pulled her thirty-eight out of her bag and checked to make sure it was fully loaded and then put it back. She knew that she wouldn't need the weapon because she had already made plans with Turk, the rec center's owner and one of her side pieces. She needed it to look like a real robbery, so he had some flour packaged up like bricks of cocaine and had hidden it in the safe.

When Trameeka got out of the Range, Bak got out and followed at a safe distance behind her. The air conditioner had been turned up too high and caused goosebumps to form on her skin when she walked inside. As soon as the clerk at the front desk saw her, she smiled. Bak suddenly became paranoid because Trameeka was a little too calm for him. He had never been a robber, and without Brightman by his side, he felt unsafe.

"Yo, why you so friendly with these mufuckas? What's up with that shit?"

"My uncle owns this place, so everyone knows who I am. Besides, the man who runs it for my uncle is your competition."

"The fuck?"

"Ah, come on, Bak, you had to have known that your dick ain't the only one I bounce on. Now, just follow my lead and let's get this over with."

Trameeka led him to the back office and put a finger over her lips, telling him to be silent. She knocked on the door lightly, and as soon as it opened, she had her thirty-eight pointed at Turk's head.

"Whoa, shit. Meeka, what the fuck you doing?"

"Just shut the hell up and open that safe and do it quickly."

"The hell is wrong with you? Janahvi knows you here doing this shit?"

"Fuck my Uncle Nahvi. I'm tired of being his damn do girl while he reaps all the benefits. It's my time to shine, and I'm knocking out anybody in my way."

"Okay, alright. I'll open the safe and give you what you came for but don't do nothing stupid with that gun you got pointed at me."

Trameeka looked at Bak and nodded her head toward the safe. As soon as Turk had it opened, he stepped to the side and held his arms up while Bak emptied its contents into the duffel bags he had carried inside. When all the bricks were secure, he pulled out a roll of duct tape and taped Turk's arms and legs to the chair he made him sit in and then turned to Trameeka.

"Yo, Meeka, why the hell we leaving this nigga alive? Shouldn't we be smoking his ass?"

"No, Bak, ain't no sense in taking lives we don't have to take. Besides, I need him to let my uncle know that I'm coming, so he might as well prepare himself."

Turk winked at Trameeka as soon as Bak turned his head to let her know he would make the call as soon as she left. They had already made plans for the clerk to untape him as soon as they pulled off. So far, Trameeka's plan had come together, but she could tell that Bak was getting antsy.

"Aye, why that shit went so smooth? I mean, that mufucka ain't even try to fight or nothing. What's up with that?"

"My uncle tells all his workers that if something like that ever happens, and it could cost them their life, they are to cooperate completely. They aren't supposed to pull their weapons or anything. He says the product can be replaced, but he can't give them back their life, but just so you know, those bags don't even put a dent in my uncle's pockets."

"Yeah, so what happens next?"

"We hit another spot and then another, but you have to understand. Each one will be harder because word will travel fast. We gotta move quickly, or we will have done it all for nothing."

"And you expect your uncle to just sit back and do nothing while we out here putting him out of business?"

"Oh, he won't be doing nothing. He will be sitting there, waiting for us to arrive, because he knows I'm coming for him too."

"You turning on your people like this makes me wonder. I mean, if you do it to them, you will do it to me too."

"Whatever, Bak. You wanna get out of my ride, because you ain't gotta come with me, but I'm doing this with or without you?"

Trameeka knew that Bak was a greedy man, and there was no way he would miss out on the opportunity she presented to him. He would be down with whatever she had planned, as long as he thought he would come out on top. He figured that he had made arrangements to take her out when it was all over. He needed to ensure that she wasn't a liability.

He just hoped that Brightman stayed in place and was ready as soon as Bak sent word.

"Nah, I ain't bout to let you go at this all alone. I got your back as long as I don't sense no bullshit."

Trameeka shook her head and drove them to their next destination, where shit would go just as smooth as the job before. It seemed strange to Bak that each spot that was hit would go without incident. He charged it to the fact that the niggas were familiar with her and that she was also Janahvi Karter's niece. One would have to be a fool to test her. Trameeka had a reputation for being ruthless in the hood and held mad respect. Bak watched as the money and product grew in size, and the bigger it got, the more at ease he became.

The thought of Alanee suddenly came to his mind, but he didn't want to say anything. He knew that it was a touchy subject, and he didn't want to piss Trameeka off, at least not yet. She had already felt some type of way about him taking Alanee to her house, but he really didn't give a damn because he was just using Trameeka anyway. He decided to track Alanee down as soon as his business in the takeover was done.

Trameeka noticed how quiet he became and asked, "What the hell you so quiet for? And don't let me find out it's because you sitting up in my shit, thinking about that bitch."

"Come on, baby, quit trippin. You the only bitch I got on my mind. Me and you bout to run the whole city. You think I'ma let Lanee's disloyal ass ruin that?"

"Yeah? Well, don't let me find out anything different because I ain't above laying you or her down."

Bak could tell by the look in her eyes that she was serious, so he knew he had to be careful. He decided that as soon as they left the next stash house, he would go ahead and reach out to Brightman. It was time for Trameeka to get out of his way, but he would soon find out she was harder to get rid of than he expected.

Chapter Nineteen

Jarell had no clue where to look for Bak because no one in the streets was talking. He may not have been a street thug, but he was well aware of the strict code the blocks enforced about running your mouth. Everyone knew to follow it; however, regardless of the no see, no hear, no tell rule, you could always find one that would break it.

Jarell approached the fiend carefully because he wasn't sure what to expect from her. The tattered jeans she wore sagged from her waist, and the dingy t-shirt looked as if it belonged to a child. The polish on her fingernails appeared as if they were painted months before and needed a quick touch up, and the closer he got to her, the more he could smell the stench coming from her unwashed hair. He tried not to vomit as he spoke to her.

"Um, excuse me. I'm looking for Bak and Brightman. Have you seen 'em around here lately?"

"Nah, I ain't seen Bak's Black ass in a couple of days, but I might know where you can find him. What's in it for me if I tell you?"

Jarell shook his head and pulled out a diamond encrusted money clip that was wrapped around several crisp one-hundred-dollar bills. He peeled one off and held it out for her to take. She snatched it quickly and put it down in her bra before he had a chance to change his mind. She thought about the bills he put back in his pocket and figured she could give him a little information and then ask for more money before she gave him any more. She licked her dry, cracked lips and was about to speak, but another voice came from behind and stopped her.

"Jarell, oh, my God. I'm so happy to see you."

Jarell turned to the voice, and as soon as he saw Alanee, he pulled her into his arms. It felt like it had been forever since they had seen each other, and Alanee felt as if her heart would beat out of her chest. He had to have known that she would never leave him willingly because she had too much love for him.

"Where have you been? What did that nigga do to you?"

"Nothing, Jarell, it's okay. I'm okay, but I have a lot to tell you. Things that you may not be ready to hear."

Jarell let her go and stared down into her sad eyes. He wanted to believe that she was it for him and hoped that whatever she would say wouldn't change that. He felt like he could trust her with his heart and was certain that she knew she could trust him too. He put his arm around her and led her to the ride, so they could talk in peace, and as soon as he got in, he opened the conversation. "Damn, baby, I really thought something happened to you. I got home and found you gone and didn't know what to do. Erica was still there, and she told me you left with that nigga, but I refused to believe that shit. She tried to convince me that you only used me to get back at Bak for how he did you. That bitch started taking her clothes off and tried to throw herself at me, but I ain't that mufucka. I finally got the truth out of her and then gave her enough money to get out of town. Bak thinks she's dead, and if he finds out she's not, he will find her and make her wish she was."

"Yeah, well, for her sake, she better hope he finds her before I do. I can't believe that she would try you after pouring her heart out to me and telling me how sorry she was. That bitch. I really believed that she felt bad for all she had done. I'm so stupid."

"Nah, Lanee, you ain't stupid. You just real as fuck, and when you care about someone, you give them the benefit of the doubt. You try to see the good in them, even when they show you the bad. You can't always believe who someone says they are. You have to believe who they show you they are. You gotta forget about her and move on. Let that shit ride because what's done is done and ain't nothing you can do to change it. Right now, I need to get my hands on that nigga."

"Jarell, before you say anything else, I need you to listen to me. You also got to promise me that you won't be mad."

"Aiight. I give you my word. Now what's up?"

"I found out about your cousin and Bak. Well, actually, I overheard the conversation between you and your father and did some investigating. I contacted her, and we came up with a plan to get Bak back for all the shit he's done."

"Look, you need to be a little more clear than what you are being. I ain't got time for no games."

"Trameeka is not really going after your father. It's all a set up. Don't you think that if one of his places had been hit, you would have heard about it by now? Don't you think the streets would have talked?"

"So, where they hittin at because I know my cousin and what she's capable of?"

"Meeka got with some of her people and packaged up bricks of flour, and they printed out counterfeit money. While Bak thinks he's putting your father out of business, the only one gettin fucked is him."

"Is my father in on this because he sure seems like he's ready to blast a mufucka?"

"Your father knows too, but he chose to keep you out of it. He said the streets wasn't the place for you."

"So, him telling me to be ready to blast was all bullshit. He never planned to involve me at all."

Alanee became silent, which gave Jarell the answer to his question. He couldn't believe that he had been so blinded by his love for her that he couldn't see everything else going on around him. He knew Trameeka could handle things on her own, but he still worried because he knew that at any time, things could backfire, and it could cost her. He couldn't allow something like that to happen, no matter what they had been through.

"Ya know, Lanee, I chose a different path than my father did for a reason, but that don't mean I don't have gangsta blood running through my veins. That shit is in me, no matter how much I try to run from it. I don't wanna end up like my Uncle Meek and die out here, but when it comes to the people I love, I'd give my very last breath. I ain't no soft ass nigga, so people need to stop playing me like I am."

"I don't think that's what they're doing, Jarell. I just think that maybe they don't want to force a lifestyle on you that you don't wanna live. They respect your choices and so do I."

"Oh, yeah, well, if I remember correctly, you didn't want shit to do with me because I wasn't a street thug like that mufucka."

"That's not fair, Jarell, and you know it. I was just playing hard to get and fucked around and fell in love with you."

"Did you fall in love with me or what my last name represents?"

"You bastard. How could you even think that of me? Ya know what? You don't even have to answer that. I'll be at the Hilton across town if you wanna find it in your heart to apologize."

Alanee jumped out of his ride and slammed the door behind her. She couldn't understand why he had come at her like that. She felt like she had proven her love to him but guessed that it wasn't enough. She would be by herself before she would let another motherfucker treat her as if her feelings weren't valid. She would give Jarell forty-eight hours to show up at the hotel, and if he didn't, she would move on and forget him, or at least try to.

Jarell sat there and quickly regretted what he had said to her. He didn't mean to take his anger out on her, but he had expected just a little more loyalty. She owed him that much.

He looked in his rearview mirror for any signs of her, but when he didn't see her, he pulled off into traffic. He was going to pay his father a visit because someone needed to put him up on what was going on, so he could handle it.

The five thousand square foot home that Janahvi and Ashley lived in was fit for royalty and only someone of their status belonged in it. Jarell knew his whole life that he had access to many riches, but he wanted to make his own way. He didn't want to be treated like one of those privileged kids that grew up on the rich side of Hollywood and never had to work. How could he have grown to call himself a man if he depended on someone else to put food on his table? He loved his parents and appreciated all that they had done for him, but it was time that they let him thrive.

He found his mother by the outdoor pool, still trying to tan her pale skin, but Ashley was a true white woman, and no amount of sun would change that. The smell of chlorine tickled his senses, as it always did, and caused him to cough. The sound startled her, and she opened her eyes and looked up at him. The sight of her only child always brought a smile to her face. Her and Janahvi had tried for many years after Jarell was born to have another child, but it just wasn't in the cards for them. Jarell was happy about it because he didn't mind getting all their love and attention to himself.

"Hello, son, what brings you this way?"

"Sup, Ma? I'm just pulling through, looking for Dad. He around here anywhere?"

Ashley could tell that whatever Jarell wanted to see his father about was serious and not in a good way. She sat up in the lounge chair and patted the chair beside her. Jarell really didn't feel like sitting down, but he would never go against what his mother asked of him, and even though she didn't ask what he wanted to talk to his father about, somehow, he felt like she already knew. Janahvi and Ashley had a solid relationship and never kept secrets, no matter how much the truth would hurt.

"Your father is down in his office, and I already know why you wanna see him, but I'm telling you, son, he is just trying to take care of what you can't."

"Ma, I don't need Pops to take a nigga out for me. This is my beef, and I'ma look like a pussy to everyone if I don't handle that shit myself. My cousin out there, already taking a chance with that nigga. What I'ma do if shit turns bad for her? Huh? How the hell y'all expect me to live with that? I'm not a child anymore, Ma. I can handle my own."

"Jarell, you're not some street thug who is used to going out there and pulling your gun on your enemies or on those people that violate you. That wasn't what you wanted out of life, and it's not something you have to do now."

"You're wrong. It is what I have to do. One day, Ma, I'ma be a father too, and I want my son to look up at me with respect, knowing that I defended the woman I love. It's my battle to fight, and I ain't about to let anyone stop me. Pops' place is here with you, not out in the streets on a murder mission because of me and my woman. He's done been there and done that. It's my turn to leave a legacy and let people know that me and anything that belongs to me is off limits."

"So, you really do love this girl."

"Yeah. I feel just like Dad told me I would feel, and every day, that shit gets stronger. Lanee is my future, and I need to step up and be the man she needs me to be, and that's a man who will do whatever he has to do to protect her. I need her to respect me and my position, but she ain't going to if I let the next man step in my spot."

"Ya know, son, you remind me so much of your father when we first started out. We went through hell to be together, and we made it. I can see the fight in your eyes, and even though I can't sit here and imagine you risking your life for someone, I know you have to do it. I don't know Lanee that well, and I know I haven't given her a fair chance, but she must be something else if she means that much to you."

"She does, and once you get to know her, you'll see why."

Jarell stood and then bent over and gave his mother a kiss on the forehead. He knew that it was her job to worry about him, but she had to believe that it would all turn out right. She was afraid of losing him to the streets, but he would never break her heart in that way. He walked away and left her to her sunbathing, so he could go talk to his father.

He climbed the staircase and walked to his father's office. Out of respect, he would usually knock, but at that moment, he wasn't feeling very respectful. He walked in and saw Janahvi sitting behind a big, red oak desk. He looked up from his computer screen and then leaned back in his chair so that he could give Jarell all of his attention.

"Why didn't you tell me that the robberies were set up? You told me to stay ready for a war you wasn't even going to allow me to fight in. Trameeka is out there, risking her fucking life for something that has nothing to do with her, and I want you to pull her out. Call it off and pull her out."

"Trameeka is a soldier, and I can assure you that she can handle what she is doing. I told you that when you have beef, we all have it, so let us fight. You know I will do anything to keep you safe, and I'm sorry I had to lie to you, but there was no other way to pull it off."

"How many houses are they supposed to hit before she brings him here?"

"Do you really think I would allow her to bring him to the place your mother and I lay our heads? Son, I've been in this game for many years, and I've had many gun battles. As you can see, I'm still here, but it didn't turn out so good for those who came at me. I would never let harm come close to home. I love your mother too much, and if something were to happen to her, it would be the death of me. I can't allow you to fight when you're not prepared."

"Dad, I've been prepared for this all my life. You raised me to be ready, and I need to show them niggas that they can't just run up on my family and not expect me to stop them."

Janahvi stood and walked to the mini bar he had in his office. He needed it for those days his mind couldn't get right. A quick shot and all things would be right in the world. He had never been a heavy drinker because he didn't like for his mind to be impaired. He needed to be able to think straight, so he didn't make a mistake. He guzzled the drink and then turned back to Jarell.

"I'll be at the warehouse when Trameeka brings him to me. He's going to think that I'm alone, but my people will be hidden in the walls. He will be expecting me to submit and to give him what he asks for. Don't be alarmed when you see your cousin with a gun to my chest. The bullets are blanks. Trameeka will help him gather what I have laid out, and right before he walks out, he will be confronted by the Grim Reaper himself. You're more than welcome to come watch the show because I promise the ending will be one you won't be expecting."

"And what position am I supposed to play once I get there? I can't sit back and do nothing."

"That's exactly what you will do. You'll sit with me, and together, we'll be counting money and packing products. I need you to act like the gangster I always wanted you to be, and everything else will fall into place."

Jarell thought about what his father said and knew that the time had come to represent the Karter name. He would do it proudly and successfully. In the meantime, he had other things to take care of. He had fucked up earlier and needed to make things right with the woman he loved, so he jumped in his ride and drove to where his heart was held up at.

Chapter Twenty

"So, where you left that nigga at?"

"Don't worry. He is in a pussy coma, and he's not waking up anytime soon."

"Oh, yeah, that pussy put him out like that?"

"Well, you know I might have put a little something in his drink beforehand, but all of that don't matter. I'm here with you now, and after tomorrow night, we won't even have to worry about him anymore."

Trameeka had been seeing Kevin for months, and he was the first man she had fucked with that made her want to settle down and be official. She had one issue standing in her way, and that was M'Baku Reynolds. When she first started seeing Kevin on the side, she never expected to catch feelings. She had always been the type of bitch that could fuck with no emotions involved, but Kevin took her to a world she had never been in, one that she didn't think she could ever exist in, but there she was, and she wanted to stay there.

She felt like Kevin would be the one man her father would have agreed with because he was just like Meek. He was a savage in the streets, and everyone knew not to fuck with him. Together, they were like Bonnie and Clyde, and their love story would be legendary.

"Ya know, I was thinking bout making an honest bitch outta you. How you feel about that? You wanna make this shit official and marry me?"

The question caught Trameeka off guard because it was one she never expected to be asked. She couldn't ever see herself as a housewife, but with a nigga like Kevin, she saw things differently.

"Damn, we ain't even put Bak's ass in the dirt yet, and you already trying to make an honest woman out of me."

"Oh, don't worry, baby. You'll still be able to mourn, just on your back while a nigga like me plants some seeds up in that garden."

"And what makes you think I wanna walk around carrying babies while you still murking bitches?"

"Don't worry. I'ma always make it home to you. I ain't neva gonna leave you in this world without me. We a team, baby, and we gonna do it all together, even death."

"Mmm, I love it when you talk nasty."

Trameeka pulled the covers back and climbed on top of Kevin. She straddled him and then filled her wetness with his manhood. He held on to her hips and dug his nails into her flesh as she glided up and down his pole. All thoughts of the mission she had planned went out the window as she enjoyed the pleasure that riding Kevin's dick gave her. She never imagined that something could feel so good. The thought of fucking with Bak again made her sick on her stomach, and she couldn't wait to rid her life of him.

Kevin was just about to bust a nut when his cellphone rang. Trameeka stopped mid-stroke, but he shook his head and made her keep going. Whoever was calling him was adamant about it because the phone continued to buzz over and over. As soon as he released his future children into Trameeka, he answered the call and put a finger over his lips for her to be silent.

"Sup, my nigga? You calling me mighty late. You aiight?"

The sound of the voice from the other end came through the phone, and Trameeka listened along with Kevin. "Man, I'm just checking to make sure we still on for the weekend. You gonna be ready to make those moves we talked about?"

"I stay ready, and you ain't got nothing to worry about. I already made a few calls, so I got some things set up, and I can assure you, the paper is right."

"Bet that up, yo. I'll check with you later on."

"Bet that. Peace out, dawg."

Kevin hung up, and together, him and Trameeka shared a laugh. She thought he was sexiest when he was handling business, and it turned her on even more. She was ready to go for another round, but he stopped her.

"Nah, baby. I think you need to head back to that nigga. You don't need to be gone too long and raise suspicion, but I'ma see your pretty ass tomorrow night, and after that, it's gonna be you and me forever."

Trameeka kissed him and got out of the bed. She hated the fact that she had to hide what they shared, but the thought of them being out in the open soon gave her some comfort. She slowly put on her clothes and left the room that Kevin had rented only a few doors down from her and Bak. She liked the fact that he wanted to be close enough to protect her, even though he knew he didn't have to.

When she got back to the room she shared with Bak, she slowly slid the key in the lock and opened the door. Bak seemed to be fast asleep, but when she shut the door behind her, he sat up and questioned her.

"The fuck you been at this time of night?"

"Damn, Bak, you scared the hell outta me, shit. I just stepped out for a minute to get some fresh air. Chill the fuck out. Your ass always on some paranoid shit. Be making me feel like you on that pipe."

"Now you know a nigga just be worried. That's all. Come on and lie down so we can get some rest. We need all the energy we can get, so we can handle that shit."

"Bak, I could handle anything thrown my way, even off of no sleep. Why you so worried? Don't tell me you trying to pussy out of the plan."

"I just wanna double check and make sure you cool going against your peeps like this. You got a lot to lose, and I need to know you mentally ready for it."

Trameeka wondered if he really cared, or was he just making sure she would still lead him to the ultimate prize?

Bak had been a selfish bastard the whole time she had known him, and she didn't expect him to ever change.

"I'm good, Bak, so you can quit asking me that. I'm not Lanee, and I don't wear my feelings. Hell, I don't even think I have feelings anymore. You can relax. I know what I'm supposed to do, and I can handle it. Now let's lay down and get that rest."

Trameeka climbed in the bed beside him, and no sooner than she laid her head on the pillow, she closed her eyes and fell fast asleep. She was exhausted and couldn't wait to finish what she had started.

The sun shining in her face woke her from her slumber. The morning had definitely come too soon, and all she wanted to do was stay in that warm bed, but she knew that she couldn't. It was time to get up and prepare for her final heist with Bak. She turned her head and saw that he was still asleep. She didn't want to disturb him, so she got out of the bed as carefully as she could and went into the bathroom where she could take a moment to be alone, but her moment wouldn't last long.

The knock at the bathroom door startled her. She unlocked the door, and Bak walked in. "You up in here with the door locked and shit. What's up with that?"

"I just needed a moment, baby. That's all. Come here and let me taste you real quick. Relieve you of that early morning hardness you got going on."

Bak smiled at the thought of pushing his dick down her throat. That first of the day morning head was always the best, and he would never turn it down. Trameeka sat on the toilet, and when Bak stood in front of her, she pulled his hardness through the hole in his boxers and gave him the last orgasm he would ever get from her. She wanted to at least send him away satisfied. He was amazed at how good his dick felt in her warm mouth. He couldn't remember her ever sucking his dick that good. It was a shame he was planning to get rid of her because he would damn sure miss her head game.

After she swallowed his seeds, the two took a long, hot shower and then called for room service. Bak was so on edge until he couldn't even eat, but Trameeka filled her stomach with scrambled eggs, turkey sausage, and hot buttery biscuits. There wasn't a caper she could think of that could ruin her appetite.

"Why you ain't eating your food, Bak?"

"I'm too hyped up about tonight to eat. Fuck around and get my stomach full, it might make me wanna lay my ass down. I need to be fully alert, so I'ma sip on this here juice and smoke me a blunt."

"Yeah, I guess that's a good excuse, but you need to hurry and smoke what you want because you ain't sparking that shit up in my ride."

Bak ignored her comment and lit his blunt. He had rolled an extra fat one and put it in his pocket, so he could smoke it afterward. Hell, he would need something to calm his nerves. The closer it got to the time for them to pull off their plans, the more nervous he became. He didn't want to let Trameeka know how he felt, so he played it off the best he could. He had done his homework on Janahvi Karter and knew what he was up against, but he wasn't sure that he was really ready. He couldn't believe that no one had come after him and Trameeka yet after all the stash houses they had run up in. He brushed it off to the fact that since she was family, Janahvi might not come at her as hard.

"What you thinking about, Bak? You mighty quiet."

Her voice broke him from his thoughts, so he decided to let her know what was on his mind. "I was just wondering why ain't nobody come after us yet. Am I missing something here because that shit don't even seem right?"

"My uncle ain't gonna miss that shit we took. You don't seem to understand how big my Uncle Nahvi really is in the game. Once we make this last hit, we'll have enough dope and money to sit back and relax for the rest of our lives. You ain't gonna ever run out of either ever again."

"Yeah, that's what you keep telling me, but I'ma have to see that shit to believe it."

Trameeka smiled at him and began to gather her things. Bak got up and followed suit. He was ready to get it over with and then find Alanee. He couldn't wait to see the look in her eyes when she saw the fortune he had amassed in only a matter of days. She would never get off his dick after that.

The two packed up the Range and pulled out into the traffic. Trameeka drove slowly through the streets because she couldn't take a chance at getting stopped by the local police, not because she was afraid of them but she didn't want Bak to get spooked. Janahvi Karter had half of the county on his payrolls, so she knew she would be exempt from any kind of indictment. She made her way to the turn off and smiled at Bak.

"Okay, baby, we are about to embark on the biggest cocaine dealer in the state so prepare yourself."

Bak looked down the long, winding road that was set in between massive forestry and pulled out his weapon. "Oh, I been ready for something like this since I was a jit. Let's do this."

He made sure his weapon was fully loaded and pushed it back down the waist of his black jeans. From the way Trameeka talked, the takeover should go down without incident, but he wasn't fully convinced. No matter how stacked Janahvi Karter was, he must have felt some kind of way about being robbed for everything he had worked so hard to obtain. Bak refused to believe he would just let them walk away with his product and money. He had wanted to take Brightman on the caper with them, but Trameeka thought it would go better if it was just the two of them. She didn't fear her uncle, and she claimed he would feel less threatened if she only brought him.

Janahvi had never been a greedy man and didn't mind sharing the wealth. He felt like there was enough to go around, so everyone could eat. Meek lost his life when he was being robbed. He tried to resist and pulled his weapon instead of letting go of what could be replaced. Janahvi swore he would never make that same mistake. He just hoped no one ever ran in on him firing because then, he would have no choice but to risk everything and fight back. He didn't care about the drugs and money as long as his family was safe.

Trameeka drove down the dirt road while Bak sat back and paid attention to his surroundings. He needed to make sure he studied everything around him just in case he had to make a quick getaway. The task at hand still felt kinda off, but he felt like he had Trameeka brainwashed and dick whipped, and she would do anything to please him.

The warehouse finally came into view, and when Bak saw it, he scrunched his eyebrows in confusion. He wasn't sure of what to think about the two-story building in front of them.

Bak pulled his weapon and put it to her temple, "The fuck is you taking me to? I thought we was going to his spot. This some type of setup or something?"

Trameeka put her hand on the gun and pushed it away. She had never been a scary bitch and wasn't about to start. Bak needed her too bad to shoot her, and if the shot would have been heard from the inside, her uncle would have sent his army out blazing. Bak wouldn't stand a chance.

"Nigga, don't you ever put a piece to my head unless you plan on pulling the trigger, and at this present moment, you ain't shooting shit. My uncle ain't a dumb motherfucker, so he would never shit where he sleeps. Ya know you could probably learn a thing or two from him while you trying to take shit you don't even know how to push."

Trameeka pulled over on the side of the road and cut the engine. Bak shook his head but put the gun away. She looked at him and then pulled her own weapon out to check it. She placed it under her shirt for easy access and opened her door. Bak hesitated at first but followed her lead.

"Don't turn pussy on me now. We've come too far, Bak. Let's finish this."

They crept up to the warehouse door, and Trameeka put her hand on the doorknob and turned it slowly. She walked in first with Bak close behind her. She couldn't lie. She was a little nervous even though she already knew what the outcome of it all would be. She guided Bak down the long hallway, and when Janahvi came into view, she put her hand on her weapon and stopped.

"There's no sense in you stopping now, Meeka. You've come this far, so you might as well finish what you started. Your father would be so disappointed."

Janahvi stood from the chair he had been sitting in, counting money, and then Jarell stood up beside him. Trameeka didn't expect her cousin to be part of the plan and hoped he didn't fuck things up because of his beef with Bak.

"My father is gone and would be proud of the woman I've become. You taught me everything I know when it should have been him teaching me instead, but he's dead and yet, you're still breathing and moving on as if he meant nothing to you. I'm doing this for him because he should be the one on top, not you."

"Ahmeek was my friend, and he made his own choices. I warned him against going, but he went anyway. I couldn't save him, Meeka. I was locked up in a prison cell. There was nothing I could do."

"You should have avenged his death."

"And what would that have done? It surely wouldn't have brought him back. It would have only started a turf war, and that could have caused all of us to lose our lives. I did right by him, and whatever you came here for today won't change that."

"Yeah, well, you know what, Uncle Nahvi? I came here to take from you what is rightfully mine. I held you down because you had a pussy for a son, and he wasn't man enough to step up and take the reins. I'm tired of you getting all the glory, so it's time I sit you down."

"And you think you'll just walk in here with that mufucka, and my pops is gonna just hand you the key to the streets?"

Jarell's presence was unexpected, but since he had spoken up, Trameeka played along.

"He's either gonna hand it to me or we gonna take it. His choice."

"Come on, Meeka, this ain't like you. The fuck this nigga done put in your head? We your family, and you gon' do us like this? Shit ain't right."

"No, Jarell, my family is six feet in the ground, and my momma went fucking crazy because she couldn't handle the pain from losing my father. You living large off of your father's success and your grandfather's fortune. You ain't had to work for nothing. I've been the one doing the work you were supposed to do because you couldn't handle the pressure."

"Aiight, well, come on, cuz, do what you came to do. This shit ain't worth our life. Take it all. Matter of fact, I'll bag this shit up for you."

Jarell began to bag up the money while his father stood by and kept a close eye on Trameeka and Bak. When all of it was in the three duffel bags they had used to bring it in, Jarell picked them up and started to walk toward Trameeka and Bak. He stopped in front of Bak and dropped the cash and then looked him in the eyes and stated, "You can have all this, mufucka, but what you ain't gonna get is Alanee. She belongs to me, and I'll kill your ass before I let her go backwards. You don't deserve her."

"Yeah, nigga, that's what you think. I'm taking my bitch back so make sure you have her shit packed when I get there. Matter of fact, you ain't gotta send her with nothing because I got enough bread to buy her a new wardrobe."

"Hold up, motherfucker. I know you don't have me up in here, robbing my own people, to help put you on top, just so you can run off with the next bitch. Nigga, you got me fucked up."

Trameeka pulled out her gun and pointed it at Bak, but he wasn't about to feel intimidated by a bitch, so he pulled out his gun too. Suddenly, all the walls in the warehouse slid open, and armed thugs stepped out and surrounded Bak, but it was the voice that he heard next that caused him the most confusion.

"Now you know I'm not about to let you take out my bitch."

"Brightman? The fuck is you doing here? You supposed to be on standby with a getaway plan, and why is you pointing a gun at me? It's they ass you supposed to be shutting down."

Trameeka let out a laugh and lowered her gun. She walked up to Brightman and stood by his side. "Thanks, Kevin, you always said you would have my back. Go ahead and take his ass out, baby, and then we can really begin our life together."

Bak couldn't believe what he had heard because he could have sworn that Trameeka and his boy hated each other. He had no idea that after the initial meeting he didn't attend, that Trameeka stormed out of, the duo's hate for each other had blossomed into much more. Bak looked around the room at all the guns pointed in his direction and lowered his. He knew then that the whole thing had been a setup and that he had lost the war.

"Last I checked, you two hated each other, so how y'all talking about being together? How you gonna do some shit like this behind my back, dawg? We like brothers. How you gonna fuck my bitch like that?"

"Nigga, I don't owe you no explanation, but since you asked, I guess I'll bring you in on the real. While you was out fucking them other hoes and leaving this beautiful woman alone, I stepped in. She deserves to be with someone who is going to be faithful to her, and since you can't seem to keep your dick in your pants, that someone is going to have to be me. Your time is finished, playa. Any last words?"

"So, you gonna kill me over Meeka's ass?"

"Nah, I'ma kill your ass for thinking you can go around town, taking shit that don't belong to you."

"Come on, dawg. I got a son that needs me. What he gonna do without me?"

"Well, I figured that since you been passing him off as mine, might as well let people keep thinking that. You got greedy, Bak, and you forgot what was important. All you care about is pussy and being a boss. Your ass don't care about sharing the wealth because you think you supposed to own it all."

"So, you gonna side with the enemy now?"

"Karter is not the enemy. Nigga would have broke bread if you would have had your mind right. The only reason Jarell had you cut off was because you got a little too big for your jeans. I'm sorry, dawg, but everything ends for you here."

"Come on, Brightman. We can take that shit and split it up."

"Bruh, you ain't got shit to split."

Trameeka stepped up in front of Bak and let him in on the secret. "Did you really think that I would go against my people for you? If you did, then you are as dumb as I thought. We ran up in those places and took bricks of flour, and the money was fake. I owe you nothing, not even my loyalty.

And as for Alanee, she was in on it too, Actually, it was all her idea."

"Nah, Lanee would never be down with anything like that. We got history together."

"Yeah, and that's what it's going to stay."

Jarell looked at his father's soldiers and nodded his head, giving them the okay to do what needed to be done. While the bullets riddled his body, Bak made peace with his creator. All he ever wanted was to be a boss, but instead of working his way to the top, he wanted to take it from someone else. The streets would not mourn him because he had never been their hero.

Janahvi looked to his son and nodded. "Go ahead, son.. Go make shit right with your girl. We gonna get the boys out here and get this mess cleaned up."

"Thanks, Pop. I owe you one."

Trameeka walked up and disturbed their moment. "Nah, your ass owes me one."

The two shared a hug, and then Jarell left the warehouse, so he could go to the one thing he cherished over everything else.

Chapter Twenty-one

Alanee packed what little bit of clothing she had taken with her to the hotel. Her heart had been broken enough, and she refused to sit around and let it be broken anymore. She really thought that Jarell was the man for her, but he had shown her different. She had given him forty-eight hours to return to the hotel, and his time was up. How could she have been so wrong about him?

She had made plans to go home and try to reconnect with her parents. She wished that she could turn back the hands of time and make better decisions. She had chosen M'Baku Reynolds over her education because she thought he was the man she would one day marry and have a family with. She had thought she was his only one for the longest time, and it hurt like hell to find out that she wasn't.

When she was done packing, she sat on the end of the bed and thought about the good times she had shared with Jarell. She didn't have a long time with him, but it was long enough to realize that she was in love with him. She wasn't sure if she would ever be able to believe in love again because if she couldn't have it with Jarell, she didn't want it with anyone. The tears formed in her eyes and threatened to fall as she thought of him. Damn, she missed him, but she refused to run after him. If he wanted to be with her, he would have to come to her.

Alanee dried her eyes and stood. She looked around the room one final time to make sure she hadn't forgotten anything. When she picked up her bag and turned to leave, she heard a knock at the door. She slowly put the bag back on the bed and stepped closer to the door. Her ailing heart beat in anticipation as she turned the knob, but when the door swung open, it wasn't who she wanted to see.

"Look, Erica, I'm on my way out and don't have time for your bullshit ass lies anymore."

"I'm not here with lies, Lanee, and I know you've heard me say it over and over, but I'm sorry."

"Yeah, I have heard you say it over and over, and quite frankly, I'm sick of hearing it, especially when I know you don't mean it."

"I do mean it, and I really need for you to believe me this time. I know that I keep making the same mistakes all the time, but I've learned from that."

"You mean the mistake of trying to fuck Jarell? That shit was real low, Erica, and not only that, but you tried to convince him that I went with Bak on my own accord when I only did it trying to protect you. If he would have known you were in the other room, he not only would have killed you, but he might have took me out too. That shit was real flaw. I felt bad for your ass, and you repay me once again with a stab in the back, but that's the last damn time I will allow you to do it. Now if you'll get out of my way, I have someplace to be."

Alanee picked her bag back up and looped it over her shoulder. She gave Erica one last glance and walked past her, but before she took too many steps, Erica told her the real reason she had shown up there.

"Alanee, Bak is dead. He was gunned down earlier, and he's gone."

The news of Bak's death hit Alanee like a Mack truck, even though she already knew it was going to happen. The thought of him being gone for good should have been good news to her, but she had spent five years of her life loving him and needed a minute to mourn. She sat back down, and Erica took it as her opportunity to comfort the only friend she'd ever had. She sat on the bed beside Alanee and held her. She wished that she wouldn't have had to bring her such bad news, but she would rather her hear it from someone who actually gave a damn.

Alanee knew that Erica comforted her, so she could try to make things up to her, but she no longer had space in her life for anyone who had wronged her. Erica didn't mean her any good, and she had to let her go. She couldn't lie. Even after all that Erica had put her through, she would miss her, but she needed to be around people who had real love for her. She pulled away from Erica and told her what she felt in her heart.

"Erica, you can't be a part of my life anymore, and nothing you say will change that. I loved you like a sister, but you treated me like the enemy. I never thought that I was better than you and never would. I never tried to outshine you or be anybody other than myself. Maybe men passed over you because they saw you for who you really were. I only wish that I would have saw it before it was too late. Goodbye, Erica."

Alanee walked out and slammed the door behind her. She had to hurry and get out of there before she changed her mind. The taxi had been waiting, and she quickly jumped inside and told the driver her destination. It felt like it took forever to get to the airport, and when she was finally dropped off, she felt even more nervous than ever. Her parents wouldn't be expecting her, and she prayed that they would welcome her with open arms. She had wanted to reach out through the years, but she was too afraid they would reject her, and that would have been the end of her for sure.

Back at the hotel, Erica sat in the room Alanee had run out of and thought about all the things she could have done differently. She had hurt someone who had done nothing but cared about her, and she regretted it. She wished that she could change the past, but since she couldn't, she decided to focus on the future. She was going to use the money Jarell had given her and enroll in the local community college and learn something to help her be somebody greater.

She had grown tired of beating herself up and trying to be someone she wasn't. She hoped that one day, Alanee would hear about the positive changes she made, and they could be friends again. She was so deep in her thoughts that she didn't hear the door open, and the sound of Jarell's voice brought her back to reality.

"The fuck you doing here? Didn't I tell you to get out of town and stay away from Lanee?"

"Yeah, you did, but I couldn't go anywhere until I at least tried to make things right with her. I really am sorry this time, Jarell, and I know I've said it so many times, but I'm for real. I'm so tired of living in someone else's shadow and trying to be like them. It's truly time to be myself and show Lanee that I can be trusted again."

"Speaking of Lanee, where is she and please don't tell me she's not here? I came as fast as I could."

"Lanee's gone, Jarell, and don't worry. She knows that Bak is no more. She took a minute to mourn for him, and then she took off."

"Where did she go? I need to go get her."

"I'm guessing she went home. Back to her parents to try and make things right between them. They wanted her to go to college, but she chose to be with Bak instead. They wanted her to do better than a drug dealer, but she didn't know any better. She really believed that he loved her, but he only wanted someone to show off. Growing up, Lanee was every high school boy's dream girl, and yet, she chose what was bad for her. She needs someone like you to love her, Jarell, and if you don't go after her, you're crazy."

"Well, it might help if you were a little more specific about her location."

Erica looked at her watch and then looked up at him with hope in her eyes. She pulled a pen from her purse and wrote down the last known address for Alanee's parents and handed it to him. "Go get her, Jarell. She needs you."

Jarell looked at the address, and without saying another word, he ran out of the hotel room in hopes of finding his one true love.

Alanee boarded the plane and found her assigned seat. She still had Bak's demise heavy on her mind and felt bad for him. She had never wished death on anyone, not even her enemies. When she called Trameeka and told her she wanted to teach him a lesson, she never meant for it to go the way that it had, and even though she wasn't the one who pulled the trigger, she felt like she was in some way responsible. She had planned on reading a book by her favorite author on the plane ride, but she was just too exhausted, so she closed her eyes and took a nap instead.

The sound of the pilot jarred her from her sleep, and when she saw that the plane had landed, her stomach felt like it had tied into knots. She got off the plane and went to the women's restroom to wash her face. She decided to touch up her makeup before leaving, and when she went in her purse to retrieve her face compact, she found Bak's cell phone. So much had been going on until she had forgotten about it. She was about to use the password she had seen him use multiple times, just so she could see what he had really been doing all those times he wasn't with her, but then she thought better of it. The things he had done no longer mattered, and so she decided to let him rest in peace. She closed up her purse and walked out right after she threw the cell phone in the trash. She knew that some things were better left alone.

Alanee got in the first taxi she saw and gave the driver her parents' address. It had been years since she had been there and prayed that they were still there. She wasn't sure what she would do if they had moved. Her mind wouldn't be at ease until the taxi pulled in front of the house she had grown up in. She paid him, got out, and walked to the door, but before she had a chance to ring the doorbell, the door opened, and eyes like hers stared back at her.

Chapter Twenty-two

Jarell rang the doorbell with confidence and prayed he didn't lose it once the door opened. He had gone to his father and asked to borrow the private jet. There was no way Janahvi could turn him down. His son was in love, and he knew that it was hard to find. He didn't want to be the reason Jarell missed out.

"So, you going to find Lanee and bring her back, but you have to understand that there could be a chance that she will turn you down. If that happens, how are you going to handle it?"

"She's not going to turn me away, Pops. I'm a Karter, and I'm kinda irresistible, so I don't think I'm going to have a problem."

The two of them shared a laugh that had been long overdue. Janahvi saw himself in Jarell and was proud to call him his son. All those years he had tried to talk him into joining the game had been fruitless, and he could honestly say that he was glad Jarell went his own way and chose to do something else with his life. He didn't need him to be a street thug to represent the family name because he did a fine job of it regardless. Him and Ashley had been skeptical of Alanee, but they recognized true love when they saw it, and what their son felt was as true as it could get.

Janahvi stood from behind the desk and picked up his phone. "Yeah, I'ma need you to get the plane ready. I'm on my way." When he hung up, he smiled at Jarell and then picked up his keys. "Come on, let me drive you to the airport."

"Yes, thanks, Dad. You can't even imagine how much this means to me."

The father and son shared some memories on the ride. Some good and some bad but all of them brought them closer. When Janahvi pulled up beside the plane, it was already running and ready to go. He was one step closer to where he needed to be. He thanked his father again, and then, the two shared a hug before Jarell got on the plane. He knew that he was making the right choice by going to her because he felt sick without her.

Jarell leaned back in the seat and reached into his pocket and pulled out the five-carat, emerald cut, diamond ring that he planned to propose to Alanee with. He knew that he wanted to spend the rest of his life with her and hoped she felt the same. He had already made arrangements to get her enrolled into college, so she could pursue whatever dreams she'd had before M'Baku Reynolds came along and ruined them. Her happiness was his, and it would always be that way. When the plane landed, he put the ring box back in his pocket and got off. His father had already alerted the airport and had him a driver waiting and ready.

Alanee didn't know it, but Jarell had already talked to her parents, so they knew that he was coming. When they heard the car pull up, they glanced at each other and smiled but didn't say anything until the doorbell rang.

"Alanee, honey, you wanna answer the door?"

"Sure, Daddy, I got it."

She didn't know who could be at the front door because as far as she knew, her parents hadn't been expecting anybody. The doorbell rang again, and she decided that somebody was about to get cursed out, but when she finally opened the door, she was speechless. She looked down at Jarell, who was on one knee on her parents' front porch. She tried to hold back the tears, but they refused to obey her.

"Jarell, you came for me. You really came for me."

"Lanee, baby, I didn't have a choice. There was no way I could have went on without you. I've already talked to your father, and he gave me his blessing, so now, I'm asking you. Will you marry me?"

Jarell opened the ring box, and more tears fell from Alanee's eyes. She put her arms around him and cried. She couldn't believe that he had come all that way to ask her to be his wife. There was no way she could refuse him.

"Yes, Jarell. Yes, baby. I can't wait to be your wife."

Jarell took the ring out of the box and slid it on her finger and then pulled her into his arms again. She was shocked that her father had kept the secret from her, but the surprise was well worth it. She was glad that she would be spending forever with a man whose love went beyond her wildest dreams. She felt like the luckiest woman in the world.

The months ahead were spent planning the wedding, and Ashley would make sure it was going to be one to remember. She was proud of Jarell and the choices he had made in his life. That was all she could have asked for. She had wished for so long for a daughter, but it just hadn't been in the story written for her and Janahvi. However, once she got to know Alanee, she became the daughter she had wished for. The Karter family was complete.

Six Months Later

Jarell stood at the front of the altar in an all-white linen suit with Gucci loafers on his feet. The smell of Gucci Guilty was coming from his skin. To say that he was a nervous wreck would be an understatement. It was the day that he had been waiting for, the day that Alanee Travis would become his forever. He still remembered the first time he talked to her and how she had dissed him. His heart told him not to give up on her, and he listened. He was so glad that he did.

When the music began, it broke Jarell from his thoughts and caused him to turn his head. His cousin, Trameeka, came down the aisle first. Her pregnant belly poked out in front of her. She was having Brightman's son, and he couldn't have been happier because he turned out to be the realest nigga Jarell had ever met. Next to come down the aisle was Erica, who had proven to Alanee that she had really changed. She was in the same college as Alanee and had a decent job. It had been hard for the two to become friends again, but once they did, their friendship was stronger than ever.

Once Erica was in place, Alanee and her father stepped out. Her beauty brought tears to Jarell's eyes and a smile to his face. She was his, and he would do all he could to make sure she stayed happy. He vowed to always love and protect her, even if he had to die doing so. Once the two of them exchanged vows, Alanee threw the bouquet, and when Trameeka caught it, Brightman went down on one knee and proposed. Somehow, Trameeka had softened up his hard side, and he was no longer out in the streets, killing people for others. He had hung up his weapon and went all the way legit.

After the wedding was over, Alanee changed into a white, crocheted, chloe, ankle length dress with a pair of Aquazzura 3D butterfly embedded heels. To Jarell, she was the most beautiful woman in the room. Him and his new wife danced to their wedding song, *All My Tomorrows*, by Kenny Lattimore. "All my yesterdays, all so blue, days spent waiting, waiting to find you. Now those sad yesterdays, they're so far behind. Another lifetime. Sign your name on my future, write your name on my heart. You're the one that I need in my life and my arms. All my tomorrows, they're all for you. For you, all of my always for all my whole life through. Baby, cause you're the one I want, I want to give tomorrow to. You'll always have all my tomorrows. They're all for you, baby."

When their dance was over, Janahvi had an announcement to go along with his toast to the new couple, "May I have everyone's attention please? I'd like to toast to my son and new daughter-in-law. Alanee, you are very welcome in this family, and my son is lucky to have you. And I'd like to say one more thing to my own beautiful wife. I am officially out of the game, and you will never have to worry about me going back in. I've washed my hands of everything because your happiness is what matters to me the most. I love you, Ashley."

The news brought tears to Ashley's eyes because she had waited so long to hear those words come out of Janahvi's mouth. They had everything they could ever want and need, and that was what mattered the most. Ashley would finally be able to rest at night because she would know that her family was safe. She couldn't have loved Janahvi any more at that moment.

The Karters were finally complete in love and in life. Some things had come along and tried to discourage them, but they fought, and love prevailed in the end. They knew that anything worth having was worth fighting for, even …

Love in the Trenches.

The End

Lock Down Publications and Ca$h Presents
Assisted Publishing Packages

BASIC PACKAGE	UPGRADED PACKAGE
$499	$800
Editing	Typing
Cover Design	Editing
Formatting	Cover Design
	Formatting
ADVANCE PACKAGE	**LDP SUPREME PACKAGE**
$1,200	$1,500
Typing	Typing
Editing	Editing
Cover Design	Cover Design
Formatting	Formatting
Copyright registration	Copyright registration
Proofreading	Proofreading
Upload book to Amazon	Set up Amazon account
	Upload book to Amazon
	Advertise on LDP, Amazon and Facebook Page

***Other services available upon request.
Additional charges may apply
Lock Down Publications
P.O. Box 944
Stockbridge, GA 30281-9998
Phone: 470 303-9761

Submission Guideline

Submit the first three chapters of your completed manuscript to ldpsubmissions@gmail.com, subject line: Your book's title. The manuscript must be in a .doc file and sent as an attachment. Document should be in Times New Roman, double spaced and in size 12 font. Also, provide your synopsis and full contact information. If sending multiple submissions, they must each be in a separate email.

Have a story but no way to send it electronically? You can still submit to LDP/Ca$h Presents. Send in the first three chapters, written or typed, of your completed manuscript to:

LDP: Submissions Dept
Po Box 944
Stockbridge, Ga 30281

DO NOT send original manuscript. Must be a duplicate.

Provide your synopsis and a cover letter containing your full contact information.

Thanks for considering LDP and Ca$h Presents.

NEW RELEASES

SOSA GANG 2 by ROMELL TUKES
KINGZ OF THE GAME 7 by PLAYA RAY
SKI MASK MONEY 2 by RENTA
BORN IN THE GRAVE 3 by SELF MADE TAY
LOYALTY IS EVERYTHING 3 by MOLOTTI

Coming Soon from Lock Down Publications/Ca$h Presents

BLOOD OF A BOSS **VI**
SHADOWS OF THE GAME II
TRAP BASTARD II
By Askari
LOYAL TO THE GAME **IV**
By T.J. & Jelissa
TRUE SAVAGE **VIII**
MIDNIGHT CARTEL IV
DOPE BOY MAGIC IV
CITY OF KINGZ III
NIGHTMARE ON SILENT AVE II
THE PLUG OF LIL MEXICO II
CLASSIC CITY II
By Chris Green
BLAST FOR ME **III**
A SAVAGE DOPEBOY III
CUTTHROAT MAFIA III
DUFFLE BAG CARTEL VII
HEARTLESS GOON VI
By Ghost
A HUSTLER'S DECEIT III
KILL ZONE II
BAE BELONGS TO ME III
TIL DEATH II
By Aryanna
KING OF THE TRAP III
By T.J. Edwards
GORILLAZ IN THE BAY V
3X KRAZY III

STRAIGHT BEAST MODE III
De'Kari
KINGPIN KILLAZ IV
STREET KINGS III
PAID IN BLOOD III
CARTEL KILLAZ IV
DOPE GODS III
Hood Rich
SINS OF A HUSTLA II
ASAD
YAYO V
Bred In The Game 2
S. Allen
THE STREETS WILL TALK II
By Yolanda Moore
SON OF A DOPE FIEND III
HEAVEN GOT A GHETTO III
SKI MASK MONEY III
By Renta
LOYALTY AIN'T PROMISED III
By Keith Williams
I'M NOTHING WITHOUT HIS LOVE II
SINS OF A THUG II
TO THE THUG I LOVED BEFORE II
IN A HUSTLER I TRUST II
By Monet Dragun
QUIET MONEY IV
EXTENDED CLIP III
THUG LIFE IV
By Trai'Quan
THE STREETS MADE ME IV
By Larry D. Wright
IF YOU CROSS ME ONCE III
ANGEL V
By Anthony Fields
THE STREETS WILL NEVER CLOSE IV

By K'ajji
HARD AND RUTHLESS III
KILLA KOUNTY IV
By Khufu
MONEY GAME III
By Smoove Dolla
JACK BOYS VS DOPE BOYS IV
A GANGSTA'S QUR'AN V
COKE GIRLZ II
COKE BOYS II
LIFE OF A SAVAGE V
CHI'RAQ GANGSTAS V
SOSA GANG III
BRONX SAVAGES II
BODYMORE KINGPINS II
By Romell Tukes
MURDA WAS THE CASE III
Elijah R. Freeman
AN UNFORESEEN LOVE IV
BABY, I'M WINTERTIME COLD III
By Meesha

QUEEN OF THE ZOO III
By Black Migo
CONFESSIONS OF A JACKBOY III
By Nicholas Lock
KING KILLA II
By Vincent "Vitto" Holloway
BETRAYAL OF A THUG III
By Fre$h
THE MURDER QUEENS III
By Michael Gallon
THE BIRTH OF A GANGSTER III
By Delmont Player
TREAL LOVE II

By Le'Monica Jackson
FOR THE LOVE OF BLOOD III
By Jamel Mitchell
RAN OFF ON DA PLUG II
By Paper Boi Rari
HOOD CONSIGLIERE III
By Keese
PRETTY GIRLS DO NASTY THINGS II
By Nicole Goosby
PROTÉGÉ OF A LEGEND III
LOVE IN THE TRENCHES II
By Corey Robinson
IT'S JUST ME AND YOU II
By Ah'Million
FOREVER GANGSTA III
By Adrian Dulan
GORILLAZ IN THE TRENCHES II
By SayNoMore
THE COCAINE PRINCESS VIII
By King Rio
CRIME BOSS II
Playa Ray
LOYALTY IS EVERYTHING III
Molotti
HERE TODAY GONE TOMORROW II
By Fly Rock
REAL G'S MOVE IN SILENCE II
By Von Diesel
GRIMEY WAYS IV
By Ray Vinci

Available Now

RESTRAINING ORDER **I & II**
By CA$H & Coffee
LOVE KNOWS NO BOUNDARIES **I II & III**
By Coffee
RAISED AS A GOON I, II, III & IV
BRED BY THE SLUMS I, II, III
BLAST FOR ME I & II
ROTTEN TO THE CORE I II III
A BRONX TALE I, II, III
DUFFLE BAG CARTEL I II III IV V VI
HEARTLESS GOON I II III IV V
A SAVAGE DOPEBOY I II
DRUG LORDS I II III
CUTTHROAT MAFIA I II
KING OF THE TRENCHES
By Ghost
LAY IT DOWN **I & II**
LAST OF A DYING BREED I II
BLOOD STAINS OF A SHOTTA I & II III
By Jamaica
LOYAL TO THE GAME I II III
LIFE OF SIN I, II III
By TJ & Jelissa
BLOODY COMMAS I & II
SKI MASK CARTEL I II & III
KING OF NEW YORK I II,III IV V
RISE TO POWER I II III
COKE KINGS I II III IV V
BORN HEARTLESS I II III IV
KING OF THE TRAP I II
By T.J. Edwards

IF LOVING HIM IS WRONG...I & II
LOVE ME EVEN WHEN IT HURTS I II III
By Jelissa
WHEN THE STREETS CLAP BACK I & II III
THE HEART OF A SAVAGE I II III IV
MONEY MAFIA I II
LOYAL TO THE SOIL I II III
By Jibril Williams
A DISTINGUISHED THUG STOLE MY HEART I II
& III
LOVE SHOULDN'T HURT I II III IV
RENEGADE BOYS I II III IV
PAID IN KARMA I II III
SAVAGE STORMS I II III
AN UNFORESEEN LOVE I II III
BABY, I'M WINTERTIME COLD I II
By Meesha
A GANGSTER'S CODE I &, II III
A GANGSTER'S SYN I II III
THE SAVAGE LIFE I II III
CHAINED TO THE STREETS I II III
BLOOD ON THE MONEY I II III
A GANGSTA'S PAIN I II III
By J-Blunt
PUSH IT TO THE LIMIT
By Bre' Hayes
BLOOD OF A BOSS I, II, III, IV, V
SHADOWS OF THE GAME
TRAP BASTARD
By Askari
THE STREETS BLEED MURDER **I, II & III**
THE HEART OF A GANGSTA I II& III
By Jerry Jackson
CUM FOR ME I II III IV V VI VII VIII
An LDP Erotica Collaboration
BRIDE OF A HUSTLA **I II & II**

THE FETTI GIRLS **I, II& III**
CORRUPTED BY A GANGSTA I, II III, IV
BLINDED BY HIS LOVE
THE PRICE YOU PAY FOR LOVE I, II ,III
DOPE GIRL MAGIC I II III
By Destiny Skai
WHEN A GOOD GIRL GOES BAD
By Adrienne
THE COST OF LOYALTY I II III
By Kweli
A GANGSTER'S REVENGE **I II III & IV**
THE BOSS MAN'S DAUGHTERS I II III IV V
A SAVAGE LOVE **I & II**
BAE BELONGS TO ME I II
A HUSTLER'S DECEIT I, II, III
WHAT BAD BITCHES DO I, II, III
SOUL OF A MONSTER I II III
KILL ZONE
A DOPE BOY'S QUEEN I II III
TIL DEATH
By Aryanna
A KINGPIN'S AMBITON
A KINGPIN'S AMBITION **II**
I MURDER FOR THE DOUGH
By Ambitious
TRUE SAVAGE I II III IV V VI VII
DOPE BOY MAGIC I, II, III
MIDNIGHT CARTEL I II III
CITY OF KINGZ I II
NIGHTMARE ON SILENT AVE
THE PLUG OF LIL MEXICO II
CLASSIC CITY
By Chris Green
A DOPEBOY'S PRAYER
By Eddie "Wolf" Lee

THE KING CARTEL **I, II & III**
By Frank Gresham
THESE NIGGAS AIN'T LOYAL **I, II & III**
By Nikki Tee
GANGSTA SHYT **I II &III**
By CATO
THE ULTIMATE BETRAYAL
By Phoenix
Boss'n Up i , ii & IIi
By Royal Nicole
I LOVE YOU TO DEATH
By Destiny J
I RIDE FOR MY HITTA
I STILL RIDE FOR MY HITTA
By Misty Holt
LOVE & CHASIN' PAPER
By Qay Crockett
TO DIE IN VAIN
SINS OF A HUSTLA
By ASAD
BROOKLYN HUSTLAZ
By Boogsy Morina
BROOKLYN ON LOCK I & II
By Sonovia
GANGSTA CITY
By Teddy Duke
A DRUG KING AND HIS DIAMOND I & II III
A DOPEMAN'S RICHES
HER MAN, MINE'S TOO I, II
CASH MONEY HO'S
THE WIFEY I USED TO BE I II
PRETTY GIRLS DO NASTY THINGS
By Nicole Goosby
TRAPHOUSE KING **I II & III**
KINGPIN KILLAZ I II III
STREET KINGS I II

PAID IN BLOOD **I II**
CARTEL KILLAZ I II III
DOPE GODS I II
By Hood Rich
LIPSTICK KILLAH **I, II, III**
CRIME OF PASSION I II & III
FRIEND OR FOE I II III
By Mimi
STEADY MOBBN' **I, II, III**
THE STREETS STAINED MY SOUL I II III
By Marcellus Allen
WHO SHOT YA **I, II, III**
SON OF A DOPE FIEND I II
HEAVEN GOT A GHETTO I II
SKI MASK MONEY I II
Renta
GORILLAZ IN THE BAY **I II III IV**
TEARS OF A GANGSTA I II
3X KRAZY I II
STRAIGHT BEAST MODE I II
DE'KARI
TRIGGADALE I II III
MURDAROBER WAS THE CASE I II
Elijah R. Freeman
GOD BLESS THE TRAPPERS I, II, III
THESE SCANDALOUS STREETS I, II, III
FEAR MY GANGSTA I, II, III IV, V
THESE STREETS DON'T LOVE NOBODY I, II
BURY ME A G I, II, III, IV, V
A GANGSTA'S EMPIRE I, II, III, IV
THE DOPEMAN'S BODYGAURD I II
THE REALEST KILLAZ I II III
THE LAST OF THE OGS I II III
Tranay Adams
THE STREETS ARE CALLING

Duquie Wilson
MARRIED TO A BOSS I II III
By Destiny Skai & Chris Green
KINGZ OF THE GAME I II III IV V VI VII
CRIME BOSS
Playa Ray
SLAUGHTER GANG I II III
RUTHLESS HEART I II III
By Willie Slaughter
FUK SHYT
By Blakk Diamond
DON'T F#CK WITH MY HEART I II
By Linnea
ADDICTED TO THE DRAMA I II III
IN THE ARM OF HIS BOSS II
By Jamila
YAYO I II III IV
A SHOOTER'S AMBITION I II
BRED IN THE GAME
By S. Allen
TRAP GOD I II III
RICH $AVAGE I II III
MONEY IN THE GRAVE I II III
By Martell Troublesome Bolden
FOREVER GANGSTA I II
GLOCKS ON SATIN SHEETS I II
By Adrian Dulan
TOE TAGZ I II III IV
LEVELS TO THIS SHYT I II
IT'S JUST ME AND YOU
By Ah'Million
KINGPIN DREAMS I II III
RAN OFF ON DA PLUG
By Paper Boi Rari
CONFESSIONS OF A GANGSTA I II III IV
CONFESSIONS OF A JACKBOY I II

By Nicholas Lock
I'M NOTHING WITHOUT HIS LOVE
SINS OF A THUG
TO THE THUG I LOVED BEFORE
A GANGSTA SAVED XMAS
IN A HUSTLER I TRUST
By Monet Dragun
CAUGHT UP IN THE LIFE I II III
THE STREETS NEVER LET GO I II III
By Robert Baptiste
NEW TO THE GAME I II III
MONEY, MURDER & MEMORIES I II III
By Malik D. Rice
LIFE OF A SAVAGE I II III IV
A GANGSTA'S QUR'AN I II III IV
MURDA SEASON I II III
GANGLAND CARTEL I II III
CHI'RAQ GANGSTAS I II III IV
KILLERS ON ELM STREET I II III
JACK BOYZ N DA BRONX I II III
A DOPEBOY'S DREAM I II III
JACK BOYS VS DOPE BOYS I II III
COKE GIRLZ
COKE BOYS
SOSA GANG I II
BRONX SAVAGES
BODYMORE KINGPINS
By Romell Tukes
LOYALTY AIN'T PROMISED I II
By Keith Williams
QUIET MONEY I II III
THUG LIFE I II III
EXTENDED CLIP I II
A GANGSTA'S PARADISE
By Trai'Quan

THE STREETS MADE ME I II III
By Larry D. Wright
THE ULTIMATE SACRIFICE I, II, III, IV, V, VI
KHADIFI
IF YOU CROSS ME ONCE I II
ANGEL I II III IV
IN THE BLINK OF AN EYE
By Anthony Fields
THE LIFE OF A HOOD STAR
By Ca$h & Rashia Wilson
THE STREETS WILL NEVER CLOSE I II III
By K'ajji
CREAM I II III
THE STREETS WILL TALK
By Yolanda Moore
NIGHTMARES OF A HUSTLA I II III
By King Dream
CONCRETE KILLA I II III
VICIOUS LOYALTY I II III
By Kingpen
HARD AND RUTHLESS I II
MOB TOWN 251
THE BILLIONAIRE BENTLEYS I II III
REAL G'S MOVE IN SILENCE
By Von Diesel
GHOST MOB
Stilloan Robinson
MOB TIES I II III IV V VI
SOUL OF A HUSTLER, HEART OF A KILLER I II
GORILLAZ IN THE TRENCHES
By SayNoMore
BODYMORE MURDERLAND I II III
THE BIRTH OF A GANGSTER I II
By Delmont Player
FOR THE LOVE OF A BOSS
By C. D. Blue

MOBBED UP I II III IV
THE BRICK MAN I II III IV V
THE COCAINE PRINCESS I II III IV V VI VII
By King Rio
KILLA KOUNTY I II III IV
By Khufu
MONEY GAME I II
By Smoove Dolla
A GANGSTA'S KARMA I II III
By FLAME
KING OF THE TRENCHES I II III
 by GHOST & TRANAY ADAMS
QUEEN OF THE ZOO I II
By Black Migo
GRIMEY WAYS I II III
By Ray Vinci
XMAS WITH AN ATL SHOOTER
By Ca$h & Destiny Skai
KING KILLA
By Vincent "Vitto" Holloway
BETRAYAL OF A THUG I II
By Fre$h
THE MURDER QUEENS I II
By Michael Gallon
TREAL LOVE
By Le'Monica Jackson
FOR THE LOVE OF BLOOD I II
By Jamel Mitchell
HOOD CONSIGLIERE I II
By Keese
PROTÉGÉ OF A LEGEND I II
LOVE IN THE TRENCHES
By Corey Robinson
BORN IN THE GRAVE I II III
By Self Made Tay

MOAN IN MY MOUTH
By XTASY
TORN BETWEEN A GANGSTER AND A
GENTLEMAN
By J-BLUNT & Miss Kim
LOYALTY IS EVERYTHING I II
Molotti
HERE TODAY GONE TOMORROW
By Fly Rock
PILLOW PRINCESS
By S. Hawkins

BOOKS BY LDP'S CEO, CA$H

TRUST IN NO MAN
TRUST IN NO MAN 2
TRUST IN NO MAN 3
BONDED BY BLOOD
SHORTY GOT A THUG
THUGS CRY
THUGS CRY 2
THUGS CRY 3
TRUST NO BITCH
TRUST NO BITCH 2
TRUST NO BITCH 3
TIL MY CASKET DROPS
RESTRAINING ORDER
RESTRAINING ORDER 2
IN LOVE WITH A CONVICT
LIFE OF A HOOD STAR
XMAS WITH AN ATL SHOOTER

www.ingramcontent.com/pod-product-compliance
Lightning Source LLC
Chambersburg PA
CBHW071209260626
47162CB00004B/1236